Santa AND THE SADDLER

CATHRYN HEIN

SANTA AND THE SADDLER
First published 2016
Copyright © Cathryn Hein, 2016

All rights reserved. Except in the case of brief quotations embedded in reviews, no part of this publication may be reproduced, transmitted or distributed in any form or by any means, including photocopying, recording, or other electronic or mechanical methods, without the prior written permission of the copyright holder.

Santa and the Saddler is a work of fiction. All names, people, places, businesses, events or incidences are fictitious and a product of the author's imagination. Any similarities to actual people, living or dead, or actual places or events are entirely coincidental.

Cover Art by Kellie Dennis at Book Cover by Design:
www.bookcoverbydesign.co.uk
Formatting by Polgarus Studio: www.polgarusstudio.com

cathrynhein.com:

About The Author

A South Australian country girl by birth, Cathryn loves nothing more than a rugged rural hero who's as good with his heart as he is with his hands, which is probably why she writes them! Her romances are warm and emotional, and feature themes that don't flinch from the tougher side of life but are often happily tempered by the antics of naughty animals. Her aim is to make you smile, sigh, and perhaps sniffle a little, but most of all feel wonderful.

Cathryn was born horse mad, which is little wonder with three generations of jockeys in the family. After scoring her first horse at age 10, upon whom she bestowed the eternally romantic name of Mysty, Cathryn spent the rest of her teenage years in equine bliss riding pony club and hunt club, and competing in eventing, dressage and showjumping until university beckoned.

Armed with a shiny Bachelor of Applied Science (Agriculture) from Roseworthy College she moved to Melbourne and later Newcastle, working in the agricultural and turf seeds industry. Her partner's posting to France took Cathryn overseas for three years in Provence where she finally gave in to her life-long desire to write.

Cathryn currently lives in New South Wales at the base of the Blue Mountains with her partner of many years, Jim. When she's not writing, she plays golf (ineptly), cooks (well), and in football season barracks (rowdily) for her beloved Sydney Swans AFL team.

Contact Cathryn via
cathryn@cathrynhein.com

or the contact form on
cathrynhein.com

You can also follow her on social media at:

Facebook:
https://www.facebook.com/cathrynhein/

Instagram:
https://www.instagram.com/cathrynheinauthor/

Twitter:
@CathrynHein

Goodreads:
www.goodreads.com/author/show/5137697.Cathryn_Hein

For Jim

One

Danny Burroughs rubbed the back of his neck as he eyed his little sister Ebony. 'A browband.'

'Yes,' she said, holding his gaze with the kind of freakish, wide-eyed intensity only the truly horse-mad possess. 'A pink and blue one. You'll have to order it.'

'Order it? Ebs, it's less than a week before Christmas. There's no way they'll get it delivered in time.'

Ebony threw him one of her 'der' looks and folded her arms. 'They make them in the shop. Just tell them it's for me and that you'll pick it up Christmas Eve.'

'Still a bit tight, isn't it?'

'A bit. But if you call in today it should be all right.' She dropped the sneery teen act to regard him from under her lashes. 'Please? I really want one.'

Danny sighed, aware he was being conned. Again. 'All right.'

Although when he'd manage to fit a visit in to O'Brien's Saddlery, he had no idea. Between his day job at Levenham

Windmills and his evening shifts at the Australian Arms Hotel, he barely had time to scratch himself let alone chase pink and blue browbands. But it was his own fault for asking Ebs direct what she wanted for Christmas instead of consulting his mum, who would at least have offered alternatives. Now he was trapped.

'Yay!' Ebs clapped her hands and bounced up to kiss his cheek before tearing off outside, no doubt to tell her pony Hobbles the good news.

Danny shook his head. Pain in the bum, but truth was Ebs had every male member of his family crooked around her little finger. Mum — who'd learned a thing or two bringing up two boys — was made of sterner stuff, but even she was susceptible to Ebony's charms when caught at the right moment.

But he loved seeing her happy, and Christmas was for kids and Ebs was still very much one, even if she didn't consider herself so now she'd reached the mighty age of thirteen. 'The accident' — as she was sometimes secretly, fondly referred to thanks to the large age gap between the Burroughs brothers and their sister — was a joy to the family and adored by all. Something Ebs was very aware of and exploited mercilessly.

Danny glanced at the kitchen clock. Almost 6 pm. Normally the saddlery would be closed by now but it was Thursday night, and in South Australia's country towns that meant the shops stayed open for late night shopping. If he rushed, he might make the saddlery before his shift at the pub.

A hundred and fifty metres or so back from the corner, where Levenham's main street connected with the highway and a petrol station flashed garish yellow and red even when closed, three uninspiring shops huddled side by side like old gossips.

The first was a charity shop — its window of red-and-green-themed clothes racks and Christmas bric-a-brac half obscured by a rusting blue donation bin. Next to it was a marine supplies. The last was O'Brien's Saddlery.

Hogging one of the four car parking spaces was a life-sized plastic display horse on trolley wheels. A pair of deer antlers were stuck to its head, while on its back — straddled and leaning back in a yee-haa pose like a bronco rider — was a Santa. Except this Santa was dressed in a blue shearer's singlet, red shorts, and wore a bush hat with corks dangling from the brim.

Danny grinned. Someone had a sense of humour.

Every parking space in front of the shops was taken. Chucking a quick U-turn, he slid into a roadside park further up the street and got out. He had five minutes to get the browband ordered but from the look of the car park, Danny didn't like his chances.

He strode for the door, pushed it open and was immediately hit by a blast of air-conditioning, some honey-voiced crooner singing 'Santa Baby', and the earthy scent of leather. He made his way to the back counter, past a grim-faced woman going through a rack of halters, and regarded the line ahead of him with frustration.

Four others waited, and from their pissed-off expressions and the way they were glancing at their watches, they'd been doing so for a while. An extremely pretty brown-haired girl was at the register, ringing up a purchase. Her lightly freckled cheeks were flushed and tendrils of hair had escaped her bun to fall around her face. She was wearing a bright red top with a cartoon reindeer on the front, the singlet's cut revealing tanned, muscled arms and very straight shoulders. She was his age, mid-twenties maybe. A quick glance at her hands revealed no rings.

Pretty, possibly single, and here was Danny looking like a dick in a Santa suit. He could kill his boss, he really could. There was such a thing as taking the Christmas spirit too far, and Jase had done it.

'Oh,' said the woman Saddlery Girl was serving, holding up a finger. 'Just one more thing.' She dashed off, leaving the girl to smile a brittle apology at the other customers.

'I won't be long.'

Danny's eyebrows lifted at the English accent, so incongruous to her freckled, summery Australianness.

'You said that five minutes ago,' muttered the bloke in front of Danny, throwing another look at his watch. He clocked Danny's stupid costume. 'Nice suit.'

Like he hadn't been hearing that all week. But Danny never saw the point in being cranky, and it was Christmas. Season to be jolly and all that.

'Thanks. Just spreading the cheer.'

He glanced back at Saddlery Girl and found her looking

him up and down. Realising she'd been caught, she raised a single eyebrow. Danny smiled and winked, delighted when she grinned broadly in return, showing off perfect white teeth and laughter-filled golden hazel eyes.

The entire room somersaulted.

Oh man, she was pretty.

The woman customer returned with a rainbow-coloured horse lead. Danny checked his watch and muttered a quiet, very un-Christmassy curse. There was no way he was going to get served in time.

He stepped out of line, catching Saddlery Girl's eye again as she looked up. 'I'll come back.'

Dismay furrowed her brow and she spread her hands in a gesture of apology.

He gave her an 'it's okay' shrug. Poor thing really did look flustered. If he was quick he might be able to call back in on his break.

Luck, though, wasn't on Danny's side. The Arms was heaving when he arrived. Added to the usual regulars and the Thursday night shopping and payday crowd, the back bar was crammed with boisterous young singles returning to Levenham for Christmas from university or new careers elsewhere. The wait at the bar was two deep and, with darkness still ages away, likely to get deeper as people finished their outside activities and wandered in for a drink or meal.

Danny endured calls of 'Nice suit!' and 'Ho ho ho!' as he pushed towards the bar. He surreptitiously gave those he knew well the finger, the others he waved off with a good-natured grin.

He lifted the timber divider and ducked through. Thanks to Jason the publican's un-brilliant idea, all the staff were in costume. Danny had drawn the short straw and scored Santa. Tall and rangy, with spiky dark hair and brown eyes, Danny was as far from Santa as a bloke could get. Barry, the grey-haired manager, had fared even worse as Frosty the Snowman, while Karen Simms — who'd been working at the pub almost as long as Barry — had drawn Mrs Claus. The only person who didn't look ridiculous was Lily, one of the casual bar staff, who was as cute as a button in her elf suit.

'No dramas?' Danny asked Karen as he passed.

'Not yet.' Karen nodded to a group of barely legal young men in the back bar. 'Might be later though.'

Danny assessed them quickly. Like Karen, experience had taught him what to look for and this lot spelled trouble. From the way Jase was observing them, he agreed.

'I'll keep a watch,' said Danny.

As suspected, the night descended into bedlam. Usually Danny could manage a quick chat to mates and regulars during his shift, but the bar was so flat out he struggled to keep up with orders. When the predicted scuffle broke out around ten, Danny helped Jase heft the troublemakers out, which earned them abuse from the drunks but plenty of cheers from rest of the patrons who'd had enough of their mouthiness and spilled beers.

His break came and went. Not wanting to leave the rest short-handed, Danny took enough time for a quick drink and a few pinched chips in the kitchen, before returning to the fray. By the time the bar closed and he'd helped with the clearing up, it was well past midnight.

He drove home to his parents' farm, exhausted and longing for Sunday and the freedom of a day to himself. It wasn't until he was climbing wearily into bed that Danny realised he'd missed the saddlery. With a groan he tapped out a quick reminder on his phone, checked his alarm was set, and collapsed into a dead sleep.

Two

Danny regarded the car park in front of the saddlery. Every space was taken, even the ones further along the road. He only had an hour for lunch and he didn't want to waste it standing in line, no matter how pretty the girl serving behind the counter.

He parked his ute and strode to the saddlery. At least this time he wasn't in his Santa suit, although his work gear — with its multiple grease stains and embroidered LW logo with his name beneath — wasn't exactly a fashion statement either.

One look at Saddlery Girl and he wished he'd worn his new cargo-pants, but Danny had woken so knackered he'd just grabbed the first pair of work duds he spied. Even harried she was pretty, whereas he just looked like a bogan.

She was standing at a rotating rack of bridles, lifting and replacing styles as the woman assessing them dithered over her choice. Today, instead of a bun, she'd caught her hair in a long thick plait that fell down the back of her sky blue T-shirt and made Danny wonder what her hair would be like loose. Glorious, he reckoned. The sort of hair a bloke would want to fist his hands in while …

He gave himself a hefty mental kick. Now was not the time for thinking about sex. He had a browband to order, a lunch to eat, and a job to get back to.

At least seven other people were browsing the shop, all casting annoyed glances in Saddlery Girl's direction. Danny was struck by an urge to tell them to bugger off and leave her alone, she was trying her best.

Although why there weren't more staff on was a mystery. And where was old O'Brien himself?

'Oh, hello again,' she said when Danny neared, then glanced around the shop. 'I'm sorry, it'll be a wait.'

'I just need to order something.'

'Does this one come in black?' asked the woman she was serving, thrusting a bridle at Saddlery Girl and glaring briefly at Danny. Clearly the background croon of 'Hark! The Herald Angels Sing' was having no effect on her mercy mild.

Saddlery Girl winced an apology Danny's way and began checking the racks. 'No, looks like we only have brown.'

'Can you get one in?'

'Not in time, I'm afraid.'

The woman pursed her lips.

'It's a lovely bridle,' said Saddlery Girl, her slightly posh accent making her sound trustworthy as well as knowledgeable. 'Made from hide that's been vegetable tanned rather than chrome tanned. It's a longer process, more expensive too, but the result is a much higher quality leather. This is tack made to last, both in terms of durability and in looks. See how fine the hand stitching is? And the smoothness, and even colour of the leather? I'm sure your daughter will love it.'

The woman fingered the bridle. Danny imagined the telepathic yells from the other browsers as they willed her to make a decision.

'I tell you what,' said Saddlery Girl, 'if she doesn't like it, bring it back and we'll order it in black.'

'Okay. Thanks.'

One down, but plenty more to go. Danny admired Saddlery Girl's bum as she walked to the counter. Her jeans hung low on her hips and though they weren't skinny-jean tight, they fitted in all the right places. So did that T-shirt. He envied the lurid green Grinch on the front, so close to her round breasts. No wonder it was smirking. He would be too, and then some.

Danny gave his head a knuckle-rub. Man, he needed to get a grip.

Ten more minutes passed, then fifteen, then twenty. After half an hour, he gave up. He didn't offer a farewell. Saddlery Girl was crouched at a display of jodhpurs with her back to him and he didn't want to make her feel bad. Besides, he'd be back after work.

Except come knock-off, that idea took it in the shorts when the boss shouted drinks after work. It was the last Friday before Christmas, and with a couple of other staff members taking off on holidays, Danny could hardly refuse to stay for at least one. Then, when the boss announced they'd all had bonuses transferred into their accounts, Danny was compelled stay for another, although this time a soft-drink.

Even drinking fast, all he had time for was a quick wash and a change into his stupid Santa suit before racing to the Arms for his shift, only to discover on arrival that Karen had been flattened by a case of dodgy fruit-mince tart food-poisoning and wouldn't be in. With the short notice and bar staff in heavy demand across the town, there was no chance of filling the shortage, leaving the usual crew — plus Jason's wife who'd been roped in to help — to pick up the slack.

Danny managed a ten-minute break to wolf down his dinner before he was back at it, and though he shouldn't have had time to think about Saddlery Girl, he did. And not just because he still hadn't organised Ebony's Christmas present.

He hadn't felt this attracted to a girl in ages. It wasn't just that she was pretty, or looked hot in jeans and a T-shirt, or had an intriguing accent. She was cheerful, even under stress, and seemed to have that can-do attitude so many people his age lacked. He admired that in a person because it was a quality he valued in himself.

The mystery was, why he hadn't noticed her around town before? And more puzzlingly, why hadn't Ebs said anything? His sister had an annoying habit of trying to pair her single brothers off and with the girl working in Ebony's favourite of Levenham's two saddleries, she was bound to know her. Yet she hadn't said a word.

If you didn't count the must-have browband.

Hmm.

It was half-past twelve when Jase told him to get his arse out of sight. Danny wanted to help clean up but the publican was adamant, and truth was Danny was dead on his feet and he had cricket Saturday afternoon. The rate he was going he'd be too owl-eyed to see his teammates, let alone bat or catch.

Unable to help himself, he took the longer route home via the main street, astonished to find the saddlery's lights still blazing. Some crazy part of Danny had him pulling to the kerb opposite, where he sat for a minute, tapping his fingers against the steering wheel and watching the window. Suddenly a slim figure appeared, quickly selected something from a shelf and hurried off.

What the hell was she still doing at work?

Danny tapped his fingers some more. Pretty bad manners to disturb someone this late but he needed to order the browband. Ebs would kill him if he failed to deliver on Christmas Day.

He stopped tapping and opened the ute door. If Saddlery Girl told him to piss off — which she had every right to — he'd cop it on the chin, but if she took the order then it was another thing he could quit worrying about.

And if it all went well, he might even find the balls to ask her out.

He jogged across the road and slowed to a walk. Seeping from under the door was the unmistakable sound of 70s rockers Slade singing 'Merry Christmas Everybody'. As the chorus came up, Slade was joined by another voice, out of tune but sung with gusto. He paused at the window and grinned as he spotted Saddlery Girl at the counter, singing loudly as she flicked through a loose pile of paper. Extracting a sheet, she belted out the chorus at the top of her voice and disappeared into the rear workshop.

Danny laughed and went to rap on the door, only to stop as a burst of common sense assaulted him. It was quarter to one on a Friday night in a quiet street in a country town, and he was a stranger dressed in a Santa suit. He'd have to be mad to think this could end well.

'Don't be a dickhead,' he muttered and headed back to the road. Halfway across the car park Danny stopped and swung back. He was meant to be helping his dad first thing, then he had cricket, but Saddlery Girl was in and he needed to order the bloody browband, and the shop was likely to be even busier Saturday morning than previous days. Two steps later Danny paused again, reversed, and with a frustrated growl, forced himself to walk on, only to halt and swing around when he heard the shop door open.

Slade had given way to The Darkness, another over-the-top British band. Danny wouldn't have had a clue, only Barry loved them and had once forced Danny to listen to an entire album one quiet Sunday morning shift at the Arms.

'You're early,' she said. 'Christmas Eve is still five —' She glanced at her watch, '— make that four, days away.'

Danny blinked in confusion. Then, remembering his costume, he grinned. She was propped against the doorjamb with her arms crossed. He studied her expression for a moment. A bit wary, definitely, but not unamused.

He spread his arms. 'Just reconnoitring for the big fella. You know, checking access, that sort of thing.' Still smiling, he walked towards the door but made sure to stop a few metres away. 'Hate to see him get stuck.'

She bent forward and peered up the street. Car headlights flashed for a moment and disappeared when the vehicle turned off. She regarded him once more. 'I thought elves looked after that sort of thing.'

'All in bed. Lazy sods.'

She studied his eyes and he tried to keep them wide. 'Where you should be, by the looks.'

The mention of his fatigue brought on a yawn. Danny smothered it with his hand and smiled when she caught the same contagion. 'Where we all should be at this hour.'

She shrugged. 'No rest for this elf. What can I do for you?'

'I need to order a browband. For a bridle.'

'I know what browbands are for.' She pointed upward, indicating the shop's signage. 'Saddlery. We're experts in that kind of thing.'

'Sorry.' He shook his head in an attempt to clear it but all he could think of was how gorgeous she looked with the servo lighting from up the street turning her hazel eyes gold-flecked and sparkling. Tiredness blushed her cheeks, but even though she looked deader on her feet than him, her mouth still curved in a smile.

He really wanted to kiss that mouth.

She raised an eyebrow, waiting. 'Any particular kind of browband?'

'Yeah.' He cleared his throat. 'Sorry. It's some sort of special thing. Leather flowers across the front.' Danny indicated his own forehead and quickly dropped his hand when he realised how stupid he must look. 'With sparkly bits.'

'I know the ones. What colours?'

'Pink and blue.'

Her grin broadened. 'Interesting choice.'

'It's not for me. It's for my sister Ebony. For Christmas.'

'For Christmas?' She glanced inside the shop, shoulders sagging, her expression suddenly giving way to fatigue. She rubbed her mouth. 'I'm sorry. There's a waiting list for those. A long one. Maybe if you'd ordered it earlier . . .'

Danny's gut sank into his Santa boots. 'You can't do it.'

She hesitated, stroking her neck as she studied him. 'It's for Ebony? Ebony Burroughs?'

'Yeah.' He held out his hand. 'I'm Danny, her brother.'

Her hand was soft and slightly greasy, from leather conditioner he supposed. The contact was brief but her grip firm. A proper handshake. Confident. He liked that.

'Beth Wells.'

'Nice to meet you, Beth.' Beth the Brit. The idea made Danny grin and quickly hide it in case she thought he was drunk. Which, in her presence, he kind of felt. Certainly he was acting the bumbling twit enough.

'And you. Ebony has mentioned you a few times.'

'She has?'

The pink flush in her cheeks deepened. 'And your brother Nick.'

'Ah. Right,' he said, understanding. Bloody Ebs and her matchmaking. Although in this instance it was hard to be cranky with her. Beth Wells was gorgeous and it looked like Danny had the jump on his brother for once.

'She's a nice girl. I'd really hate to let her down.' Beth scraped her teeth over her bottom lip and glanced again towards the back of the shop.

'It's okay. If you can't do it, you can't do it. Ebs'll survive.' Although Danny wasn't sure the same could be said for him.

She sighed. 'I'm really sorry. They're not difficult to make, but they are fiddly and time-consuming, and there are already five others on the waiting list. I'm going to have to work right through to get those made as it is. With the shop so busy there's simply no time during the day, plus I have repairs, shelves to stock. Sleep when I can fit it in.'

'It's fine.' Danny smiled to show he meant it, then frowned. 'Hang on a minute, did you just say *you're* making them?'

'Who else?'

'I don't know. John? He still owns the place, doesn't he?'

'He does, but he's currently indisposed. There's me or nobody.'

'So you're . . .'

'Manager, dogsbody, saddler.' She crossed her hands over her chest. 'You name it, I'm it.'

'Saddler?'

Beth gave a single nod. 'Qualified saddler.'

'Wow.'

'Wow indeed.'

Danny glanced at his ute and back at Beth. He was knackered but she looked worse. Still heart-stoppingly pretty though, and it was Christmas. Time of goodwill, peace among men and all that.

'I don't suppose . . .' Danny shook his head. Stupid idea. Dumb. 'Thanks for talking to me. I'll let you get back to work.'

'What?'

'Nothing. Don't worry about it.'

She stepped towards him, frowning. 'Come on, what?'

'It's stupid.' But Beth was looking at him, puzzled and tired and lovely, and it made Danny's mouth go in a completely different direction to his head. 'I don't suppose . . .'

Beth raised her eyebrows and twirled her hand in a 'spit it out' motion.

'You'd like a helping hand from Santa?'

Three

There was a crazy man at the shop door. Or a drunk, given his offer. Beth couldn't quite figure out which. Danny Burroughs was cute though, as his sister Ebony had mentioned every time she'd come into the shop.

'You want to help me.' It was more a statement of disbelief than a question.

'Yeah.' He scratched the back of his neck and grimaced. 'Like I said, stupid.'

Stupid? Maybe. It really depended on his motives, but from his embarrassment Beth was sure he'd meant well. She'd met his sister and mum Judy several times now and they seemed like nice people. Solid country folk, friendly and no-nonsense. Ebony was horse crazy. Beth could remember being the same at her age, and hadn't minded indulging the young girl's obsession.

She frowned at him, still uncertain. 'You mean . . . now?'

'What? No!' He cleared his throat. 'I mean, not unless you're really desperate.'

Oh, Beth was desperate all right. She hadn't been joking about sleeping only when she could squeeze it in. With the backlog of orders, repairs, and five hundred other things that needed doing, she'd be fortunate to get a few hours between now and close of business Christmas Eve.

She gnawed her lip, a habit she'd had from childhood when hit by indecision. 'Do you have any saddlery experience?'

'Only with Ebony's stuff.'

'Use a sewing machine?'

Danny shook his head then, grinning, he lifted an arm to strike a muscle-man pose, and wiggled an eyebrow. 'I can lift heavy things.'

Beth looked dubiously from Danny to his arm and back again. At her nonplussed reaction, Danny's grin faltered. Glancing at his arm, he caught the unflattering droop of his Santa suit sleeve and, reddening, jammed his arm back to his side.

He really was cute. Slightly bonkers, but cute.

'Lifting heavy things could be a handy skill.' And she did have stock that needed checking and shelving. Boxes of the stuff.

Beth rubbed her mouth, considering. The shelves wouldn't repack themselves, and empty shelves didn't sell goods. This time of year even the most determined list-following shopper could be tempted into an impulse buy if items were displayed properly. Takings were definitely up — Grandpop had told her so when she phoned the cash reconciliation through at each close of day — but she needed to keep it that way. Her grandparents were having a hard enough time as it was. Beth couldn't let them down.

'Do you seriously want to help?'

Danny held her gaze with soft brown eyes that were made even lovelier by the darkness of his lashes. Eyes that made her think of delicious things, like chocolate and coffee and the rich dark soil of home.

'I seriously want to help.'

She broke into a smile. 'An offer from Santa. How could a girl refuse?'

'Coffee,' said Beth, pointing to the cheap pod machine she'd bought a few days after arrival when she decided she could no longer cope with Grandpop's awful instant. 'There's milk in the bar fridge over there, mugs on the shelf above. Sugar as well.'

They were in the rear workshop. At least Beth was. Danny was hovering in the narrow area behind the counter, as though undecided whether he'd made a mistake and crossing the threshold between the two spaces would seal it.

Beth leaned against the timber bench that ran the length of the side wall. 'Changed your mind?'

'Not me. Just giving you a chance to.'

'Why would I do that?'

He scratched at a spot above his left ear. 'Because it's late, you don't know me. Pretty girl alone.'

'Are you telling me you're dangerous?'

'What? No!'

She narrowed her eyes and sucked air through her teeth, feigning doubt. 'You are wearing a Santa suit.'

'It's for work. I pull beers at the Arms. Publican wanted to get into the spirit of things.'

Beth lifted a savage-looking pair of shears off the bench and twisted them left, then right, before opening the sharp blades and rapidly closing them in a nasty sounding snip. The jolt from Danny made her want to laugh.

'Don't worry about me, I can take care of myself.'

'Yeah.' His Adam's apple bobbed as he swallowed, eyes fixed on the blades. 'I'm sure you can.' He breathed in and with a last wary glance at the shears, stepped into the room. 'So, what can I do?'

'How about making us both coffee? We're going to need it. White, two sugars.' With that, Beth set down the shears and strode to the back of the room and the table where she'd been painstakingly crafting tiny leather rosettes from red and white leather strips for another browband order.

It was an annoyance as well as a thrill to see them become so popular. Three weeks ago, looking for something to occupy herself one Saturday evening in her grandparents' house, she'd played around with a few browband designs and come up with a flowery green and gold version. Not thinking too much other than it was quite appealing, and ignorant those were Levenham Pony Club's team colours, Beth put the browband on display in the shop only for it to be immediately snatched up by an ecstatic pony clubber.

From there the uber efficient world of teenage communication took over. Within a week, Beth was fielding orders from every horse-mad teenage girl in town, along with their relatives. Which would have been wonderful had she the time to make them. Even factoring in the Christmas rush Beth hadn't expected to be this busy or exhausted, but the last two weeks had been insane. Now all those orders, along with everything else, were biting her fair on the bottom.

At least it would only be for a little while longer. The moment her grandparents returned from Adelaide, she'd be farewelling Levenham and heading back to New South Wales and the relative calm of her own life.

Assuming she had a job to return to. Beth wasn't exactly in favour at her work at the moment, but the older she grew the more she realised that family mattered more than any job, and her grandparents needed her. The timing was unfortunate but her employers could either like it or lump it — she was doing this.

It only seemed like moments after Beth sat down that Danny placed a mug in front of her. She took a sip and nodded in approval. 'Not bad.'

'We do coffee at the pub.' He took a sip of his own drink and looked around. 'What else needs doing?'

Beth reached for a curved awl and felt a twinge across her shoulders, and wondered if a massage wouldn't be too much to ask. Every part of her ached from overwork and fatigue. She smiled to herself as she remembered Ebony's claim that her brother was handy as well as handsome. Beth guessed she wasn't thinking along quite those lines though. Then again, the young Miss Burroughs had been quite unsubtle about her matchmaking, and farm girls tended to learn about the birds and the bees earlier than most.

Beth tipped her head towards the stack of boxes and loose packets that had been accumulating near the back wall over the last few days, and she had yet to sort. 'You could unpack those for me.' She pointed to the hooked rail above the bench. 'That clipboard hanging there has the order forms. I taped the invoices to the boxes so they wouldn't get lost, and the others should be inside the packets. If you could match them up as you go, that'd be ace.'

'Easy enough.' After retrieving the clipboard, Danny set down his mug and crouched by the first box. 'Box cutter?'

'Bench.'

He fetched it and bent to cut open the first box, giving Beth an impressive view of his rear. Santa suit or not, it was a pleasing look, but with his broad shoulders, easy grin and dreamy, thick-lashed brown eyes, Danny Burroughs was pleasing to look at all over.

Beth observed him surreptitiously as she sewed, checking that he was matching the orders, invoices and stock properly. From his efficiency, this wasn't the first time Danny had done something like this. Perhaps he helped with deliveries at the pub or his other job.

A few minutes was enough to leave Beth confident she didn't need to supervise, and free to concentrate on her rosettes. Why she hadn't chosen a simpler design was a mystery. There were easy ways to create leather flowers, using layered cut-outs, notched, doubled-over strips or simply wound thongs, but no, Beth had to choose a painstaking method that involved stitching individual coloured petals together to create tiny rosettes. The rosettes were then fitted with coloured crystal centres before being glued and stitched to a nylon strip, which was then itself glued and stitched into a specially tooled leather browband.

With each browband requiring fifteen rosettes, and with every customer demanding personalised colours and sizes, it was a nightmare.

When she'd completed another three, Beth shook her hand to ease the cramp and lifted her arms to stretch.

'You okay?' asked Danny. He was hunkered down next to an open box, clipboard on one knee, pen tucked behind his ear

'Uh huh. Just aches and pains from fiddly work.' She smiled his way. 'How are you getting on?'

'Just about done.' He pulled the pen from behind his ear, marked up an invoice, and rummaged in the box for the next items. 'I could probably stack some of this for you. Easy stuff, like the brushes and hoof picks.'

'Could you?'

'Sure.' He winked cheekily. 'Santa's here to help.'

The wink did something tumbly to Beth's insides. She quickly snatched up a leather petal and began pleating the end, lowering her face so Danny wouldn't see how affected she was. God, he was attractive. Not only attractive, but nice too. Why didn't men like that hang around the saddlery where she worked back home? Not that she'd get to see them if they did. Beth spent most of her days in the workshop slaving over the many boring or unpleasant repairs that the owner Gus couldn't be bothered with, while his wife Mandy manned the counter and their daughter Elise meandered around the shop floor, doing as little as possible.

Beth glanced up to find Danny still looking at her.

'What?' she asked.

'Nothing.'

For a moment it seemed all they could do was stare stupidly at one another, then a sudden yawn had Beth breaking eye contact and she quickly covered her stretched mouth. The yawn was enormous.

'Now you've done it,' said Danny, covering his own yawn.

'God, sorry. I'm so tired.'

He looked her over. 'Why don't I shelve this stuff and we call it quits?'

Beth regarded her work surface. 'I still have six more rosettes to make.' Plus the rest of the gluing and stitching. The thought made her feel even more fatigued and disconsolate. How was she meant to get this done and look after the shop?

'You keep going much longer and you'll only make errors.' Danny nodded at her tools. Almost all of them had a sharp point or honed edge. 'Or end up hurting yourself.'

Beth toyed with the petal. He was probably right. Even now she could see the stitching on the rosettes was a little uneven. She was very, very skilled at her trade and proud of it, and accepting substandard work had never been her ethic. Long order list or not, Beth wasn't about to start.

'Okay. A few more and I'll close up.'

'Good girl.' He returned the clipboard to its hook, then

hoisted up the first of the boxes. 'Santa's going stacking. You be careful or I'll send my elves after you. They're lazy but can be nasty little buggers when necessary.'

She laughed. 'I'll try.'

Beth watched until he'd disappeared into the shop, then shook her head and resumed work. When Danny returned, he'd pulled down the top half of his suit and knotted the arms around his hips. He wore a mottled dark grey T-shirt that fitted his athletically lean body and showed off muscular biceps. Beth kept her head down but slyly watched the way his arm muscles flexed and bulged as he hefted another box, then admired the view of his shoulders from the rear as he headed back out.

Two more boxes followed before Danny stood in front of her workbench and leaned across to switch off her lamp. 'Time's up.'

'Hey!'

'You need sleep.'

Beth glared at him. 'Who made you my mother?'

'Beth, it's quarter to three in the morning. You can't keep going. And you promised.'

She blinked. Her eyelids felt sandblasted, her hand an arthritic wreck and her body boneless, but she still felt a protest was in order. Switching off her lamp was taking liberties, even if he was right. 'It wasn't a promise.'

'Okay, so you agreed. Close enough.' He held out a hand. 'Come on.'

Beth regarded it for moment, then with a sigh grasped it and let Danny haul her up.

Danny planted his hands on his hips and looked around. 'What do we need to do?'

'*We* need to do nothing. *You* can clear off.'

'Not happening.'

Beth made a choked noise. The man was becoming far too big for his Santa boots. 'Really?'

'You'll only sneak back to work.'

Which was possibly true, but that was her problem, not his. Beth planted her own fists on her hips but Danny ignored her.

'So where's the alarm? There's an alarm, isn't there?'

Beth said nothing.

He regarded her for a moment then to Beth's surprise he grinned. 'You think that look will get rid of me? I've a teenage sister. Your sulk has nothing on hers.'

'I'm not sulking!'

'Much.'

'You,' she said, thrusting a pointed finger at him, 'are the most annoying Santa ever.'

'Yeah, I'm a disgrace to my suit.' The grin turned cheeky as he lazily raked his gaze over her body. 'You know how I said I can lift heavy things?'

Beth's eyes widened. Palms out, she took two hasty steps back. 'Don't you even think it.'

Danny shrugged. 'It's either that or you start locking up.'

'Bad Santa. Very bad Santa.'

'Nope. Santa with an ulterior motive.'

'Which is?'

'I need a browband for my sister and it won't get made if you're dead on your feet.'

Beth sniffed and lifted her chin. Despite her exhaustion she was enjoying this. Danny Burroughs was *fun*. And nice and cute, and . . .

She really needed to stop that. Like now.

Beth lifted her chin even higher. 'It won't get made at all if you keep acting like a bossy boots.'

'You want to see me get really bossy?' He feigned sizing her up again. 'Fireman's lift I reckon. Over the shoulder, but I promise to be gentlemanly and refrain from patting your bum.'

Finally, she laughed. 'All right, you win. But only because you helped.'

Beth checked the rear door locks and headed to her bag, stowed in the same cupboard that hid the safe. The day's takings and cash float were already safely away. All she needed to do was grab her phone from its speaker dock, turn off all the lights, set the alarm and secure the front door.

Danny dogged her steps until they both stood in front of the shop. A light northerly was blowing and the summer-scented night was warm and clear. Stars embroidered the sky like silver sequins. For a moment, they both stared heavenward as though mesmerised.

'Thank you,' said Beth, meaning it. 'For helping, and making me leave.'

'You're not gone yet.' He scanned the car park. 'Where's your car?'

'Don't have one. I walk.'

'You what? Oh, no, no, no. You are *not* walking home.'

Beth folded her arms and propped on one hip. 'It's two blocks.'

'I couldn't care less if it was two doors. I'll drop you home.'

'You've done enough.'

'Fireman's lift.' He leaned close. 'With a bum pat.'

'All right, all right.' Beth dug a finger into his chest. 'But only because I'm too tired to fight back.'

She gave him directions, noting the way he handled the ute. Danny had the casual expertise of a man who's been driving since boyhood, most likely because he had. Even Ebony had said she was allowed to drive her parents' farm vehicles. Beth had envied how carefree and rich her childhood sounded, how close and loving her family. Torn between warring parents, Beth's had been nothing like that.

Danny pulled up at the front of her grandparents' simple limestone house and undid his seatbelt.

'I'm fine,' Beth assured, staying his arm.

'No doubt you are. I'm still walking you to your door.'

Rolling her eyes, Beth alighted and headed towards the house, digging in her bag for her keys as she went, long-striding Danny on her heels.

He held the screen door open for her as she fitted the key and pushed the main door open. Once again she'd failed to leave the hall light on and the house loomed dark and desolate.

'Okay?' he asked, when she hesitated.

'Yes.' She smiled to hide the sudden rush of loneliness. 'All good.'

'Good. Now get some sleep and I'll see you tomorrow.'

Beth was halfway inside when his words clicked. 'Hang

on.' She whirled around. 'What do you mean tomorrow?'

But Danny was already jogging down the porch stairs, hand held up in farewell, Santa costume arms bouncing as he went.

It was late morning and Beth was helping a customer with a Drizabone coat fitting when Danny sauntered into the saddlery. He was wearing snug-fitting cricket whites and carrying a plastic bag in one hand and a lidded, tall paper cup in the other.

He nodded politely at the customer before smiling at Beth and holding up the bag. 'Bought you a present.' He pushed the drink towards her, encouraging Beth to take it. 'Orange juice.' Then he rummaged in the bag, releasing the aroma of something deliciously greasy that made Beth's stomach rumble. A plastic container emerged. 'Some of Mum's fruit salad for later.' The container disappeared to be replaced with a grease-stained paper bag. 'Egg and bacon sandwich.'

Beth opened her mouth, closed it and shook her head. 'Bad Santa.'

It was a ridiculous thing to say but he'd left her so flummoxed it was all Beth could think of.

The customer eyed her with confusion but Danny only laughed, picked up her free hand and hooked her fingers around the bag. 'Eat, or I really will be a bad Santa.' He glanced at the other customers. 'I'll leave you to it.' Then he nodded at the bag. 'Don't forget to eat.'

Beth watched him leave with a kind of awe. First Santa, now a knight in white nylon armour. The thought of what he might surprise her with next was exhilarating.

'Seems a caring young man,' remarked her customer as she peeled off the Drizabone.

'Yes,' replied Beth, holding the bag tight to her belly as she watched Danny jog to his ute through the big shop window. 'He is.'

And such a terrible shame she'd only have him for Christmas.

Four

To Danny's great relief the Arms was a bit quieter Saturday night for his shift. The excitement of the start of what would be the Christmas–New Year break for many had worn off, and with the glorious December weather locals were staying home, enjoying backyard barbecues with family or friends, or trekking south to Port Andrews for beachside fun.

Whatever people were doing Danny was grateful they were doing it away from the Arms. Knackered didn't even begin to describe his bone-weariness, yet he also felt strangely buzzed and expectant, and the feeling made his feet float and his grin come easy despite his tiredness.

Beth was the cause. Pretty, hard-working, good-humoured, talented and sexy Beth Wells. Danny didn't know anything about her except that she was John and Lynn O'Brien's granddaughter, and that his head was full of her, his heart too. A few hours in her gorgeous presence and he'd come down with a fully-loaded crush. He was as happy as . . . well, Santa in a sleigh steering a dozen red-nosed reindeers around the world.

Merry Christmas, Danny-boy.

The thought brought on another dopey grin that had Barry eyeing him warily.

'What's up with you, Santa? You been on the elf juice again?'

'Just being jolly. You should try it one day.'

Which earned Danny a hmph and another dodgy glance from Barry, but didn't affect his mood one bit.

Late in his shift when he had a spare moment, Danny picked a couple of packets of nuts from the rack and paid for them, along with two bottles of beer. He didn't know if Beth drank beer but she looked like that kind of girl. What she looked like was *his* kind of girl, and Danny had every intention of making her that. Tonight would be good, but he'd take tomorrow. After all, she was tired and distracted and a bloke couldn't rush these things.

He wanted to though. Badly.

As soon as knock-off came, Danny was out of the Arms and shooting for O'Brien's.

'Santa to the rescue,' he announced when Beth unlocked the door. He held up the beers and nuts. 'Sustenance.'

She leaned against the jamb with her arms folded. 'What are you doing here?'

Danny studied Beth's face, trying to figure out her mood, whether she was pleased or the defensive folded arm act was just that — an act. 'I've come to help?'

He cringed at how the rising inflection made him sound like a girl.

'Danny, you played cricket today, and you've obviously

done a shift at the pub.' She indicated his Santa suit. 'I'm fine, go home. There's no point both of us ending up exhausted. I was planning to finish up soon anyway.'

He shrugged. 'So I'll hang around and take you home.'

Beth pinched the bridge of her nose and shook her head. 'You do realise Santa is meant to come only once a year and not every night?'

'Ah, but Beth, you should know by now that this Santa never plays by the rules.'

The music playing in the shop changed. Danny didn't recognise the song but it was loud and thrashy, the sort of music and volume that someone trying to keep awake would use.

Danny's eyes narrowed. 'You weren't going to go home, were you?'

She dropped her hand and sighed. 'No.'

'In which case,' he said cheerfully, 'we definitely need to share a beer.'

For a good moment Beth simply glared, but it was a fake one. The corner of her mouth kept twitching upward. 'You're not going to leave, are you?'

Danny grinned. 'Not a chance.'

Beth kept up her glare for a few seconds longer before flapping her arms and giving in with a huffed, 'Come on then.'

Not giving her a chance to change her mind, Danny strode straight to the workshop while Beth relocked the door. By the time she arrived, he had the tops twisted off the beers and the salted cashews and macadamia nuts open on the bench.

Danny handed her a beer and tapped the top of his stubby against hers. 'To Christmas and you getting some sleep.'

'God, yes.' She eyed him as she drank to the toast. 'Did you win?'

'Cricket? Yep, by three wickets. I made thirty-eight.' Danny didn't feel it necessary to add that he'd been so busy daydreaming about her that he'd also dropped two catches, much to the disgust of his teammates.

'This is limited over cricket?'

'Yeah, I used to play grade but these days I don't have the time. Too busy working.'

'Impressive all the same. How was the rest of your day?'

'Good. Uneventful. Pub was a bit quieter tonight. Did you eat your sandwich?'

'I did. Cold unfortunately but it still tasted good, and the fruit salad was a great pick-me-up. Thanks for that. It was kind of you to think of me.'

He took another swig of beer. 'What did you have for dinner?'

Beth's eyes darted away from his. 'I managed a couple of biscuits.'

'A couple?'

'One.'

'Man, that's terrible.' He pushed the nuts towards her and lifted his eyebrows when she made no move to take any. 'Eat. You can't work without fuel.'

'You're bossy.' But she took a handful of cashews and started popping them in her mouth anyway.

'Someone has to be. May as well be me.'

Though she complained and accused him of being a bossy boots and a bad Santa, Danny made sure she ate every nut before letting her return to work. The beer probably hadn't been a good idea given her empty stomach, but it was likely she hadn't been keeping her fluids up either and it was better than nothing. He made her a mug of coffee to compensate for the alcohol and to provide an extra boost of sugar.

'Right,' he said, setting Beth's mug in front of her and clapping his hands together. 'What can I do?'

For a moment Beth stared vacantly at the counter then she blinked and shook her head. 'I'm not sure there's much you can do. Talk to me? Keep me awake?'

'I can do that.'

Although Danny would have preferred a more active method of keeping Beth awake than just talking, it was the perfect way to learn more about her. And Danny wanted to know everything.

There was a stool at the end of the bench. Danny dragged it to a spot near her worktable where he could lean against the wall, and settled down. He watched, fascinated, as she punched holes in a leather petal, gathered the ends and then loosely sewed them until the leather formed a delicate cup. Using different rows of colours, she then sewed the petals together until a perfect flower formed. Though her lamp brightened the bench, such was the intricacy of the work, Beth had to hunch over it.

No wonder she was tired. Danny could feel the toll of

tedium and strain of the fine work from simply looking.

'So this is your grandfather's saddlery,' he said.

'Yes. And Grandma's. They own it jointly.'

'But you're English?'

'Actually, I was born in Australia. In Adelaide, but my dad's a Brit so I'm both.'

Danny blinked. 'Your accent's from your dad?'

She looked up, laughing softly. 'No. We moved to England when I was five. I did all my schooling there, and my apprenticeship. I only moved back to Australia sixteen months ago, when Mum decided to come back. What about you? I'm betting a born and bred Levenham local. In fact, I bet you can trace your ancestors back to settlement. Am I right?'

'Not quite settlement but the Burroughs have been here a while. I went to St Joseph's Primary and then on to Levenham High, same as Mum and Dad and my grandparents.'

'After that?'

'Like you I got an apprenticeship. Metal fabrication.' He shrugged. 'Been in the same job since. The boss is decent bloke, the money isn't too bad, and I like what I do.'

'And what's that? What you do, I mean.'

'I build windmills. You know, that pump water. Other stuff too, but mainly that.'

She set down her awl and flexed her hands as she regarded him with interest. 'Do farmers still use those?'

The question didn't surprise Danny. A lot of people were sceptical when they heard about Levenham Windmills.

'Yep, and with good reason. Windmills are cheap and last forever — well, not forever, but a long time. Plus they pump day and night whenever there's wind, and with a well-engineered mill it doesn't take much of that for it to work. There are no power bills, bugger-all maintenance — with ours at least, can't speak for our dodgy opposition — and you can install them most places. Hard for stock to damage them too.'

'You sound proud.'

He liked the smile in her voice, the approval, and his chest swelled with it. 'I suppose I am.'

He let her carry on working for a few minutes before talking again.

'Why saddlery?'

She looked across at the bench and its tools and the racks of leather in varying shades of colour and thickness. 'I don't really know. It wasn't something I set out to do, like a life-long passion or anything, but I do remember coming here when I was little, visiting Grandpop. I loved the smell of the place and the feel of the leather. It was earthy, real. Comforting.' She shook her head and looked back down as though embarrassed by the words. 'Mostly it was because I wanted to be around horses. I was even madder than Ebony about them when I was young.'

'Do you have your own?'

'No. I never have.'

Alerted by something in her tone, Danny leaned forward. 'Why not?'

'It just never worked out. There was a riding school not

far from where we lived though. That's where I spent most of my early teenage years. I used to help out in exchange for riding lessons. They had a saddler there, a lovely old man named Angus who took me under his wing when he learned Grandpop was in the same trade.' Her head tilted at the memory, and her voice became wistful. 'He used to let me sit with him when things were bad at home.'

'Bad at home?'

'Oh, nothing.' Beth waved a hand. 'Just Mum and Dad arguing. I bet you spent your childhood riding motorbikes around the farm and playing sport.'

Danny didn't miss the abrupt change of subject but let it slide. There'd be time for probing that part of her life later. He leaned back against the wall. 'Pretty much. Nick and I were competitive buggers. We'd race each other on anything — quads, pushbikes, poddy calves. Dad was never too happy about that though.'

She laughed, which was what Danny had intended.

'Did you ride bulls too?' she asked.

'Nah, only calves and the occasional heifer. So I guess the plan is for you to take over here?'

She frowned at him. 'What makes you think that?'

The change in tone had his skin prickling. He eased off the wall, not liking the way she was looking at him either, sort of pityingly. 'Well, you're a saddler . . .'

'With a job already. I work at a place in Dural — that's northern Sydney. Near Hornsby? Berowra?'

He shook his head. Danny had no clue about Sydney. He'd been there a couple of times to visit and once to catch a cricket test at the Sydney Cricket Ground, but that was his limit. Besides, he couldn't give a rat's arse where Dural was. All that mattered was that it wasn't here and here was where she belonged.

Beth was still regarding him with that soft, pitying look. 'This is only temporary, until Grandpop is home from Adelaide. My great aunt — Grandma's sister — has been sick with pneumonia. Grandma went up to look after Barbara after she came out of hospital, but then Grandma had a fall and broke her hip, and Grandpop had no choice but to drive up and care for them both. He was going to close the shop but I offered to look after it, and here I am. Grandpop said that, all going well, they should be home sometime before New Year. I hope so. I'm not sure my employers will let me take any more leave, even unpaid.'

'Right,' Danny said, and knew he sounded pissed off, but he *felt* pissed off. In front of him sat the girl of his dreams and she was going to disappear in a matter of days. It was as if Danny had been given the best Christmas present in the world only to have it snatched out of his hands just as he was unwrapping it.

'This job in Dural, do you like it?'

'It's okay. It's a big shop in a really horsey area so I'm kept busy, and it's close to Mum. She lives near Windsor with her partner Curtis. He's in the RAAF and stationed at Richmond. They met in England when he was posted there and then when he was posted back to Australia she came too, and I followed.'

Danny digested her words, noting she sounded nothing

like he did when he talked about his job. There was no pride or excitement in her voice, more resignation, as if it was the best she could do.

Yet this was the same girl who cared enough about her grandparents to take leave from her job at the busiest time of the year to look after their shop. And create more business by working her guts out to fulfil orders for browbands she'd designed for the fun of it.

That took passion, loyalty . . . things it seemed clear she didn't feel for her Dural job. And with that awareness hope glimmered.

Beth belonged here. She just didn't realise it yet.

All Danny had to do was show her the way.

Five

Beth was vacuuming the shop floor to the strains of 'O Come, All Ye Faithful' early Sunday morning when, on cue, Danny waltzed in carrying his Santa hat.

She gave him a look and kept vacuuming, but the moment she'd spotted that smile her heart had thudded and excitement had curled in her belly.

Danny didn't seem to mind, he simply leaned against the wall and watched her. Though she tried to resist, Beth couldn't help her sly glances. Whether in a Santa suit or cricket whites, Danny was good-looking but today his attractiveness was borderline ridiculous. The man wore jeans and a polo shirt like a catalogue model, his folded arms causing his biceps and chest muscles to swell behind the dark green fabric. His hair, still slightly damp, stood in dark spiky tufts and his eyes had the glittery look of someone enjoying themselves hugely.

With a last sweep near the counter, Beth turned off the machine and headed into the workshop to stow it away.

Danny, as expected, followed.

'Sleep well?' he asked.

'Not as well as I hoped, unfortunately.'

Beth's sleep debt was now so gargantuan it was as if her body had forgotten what unconsciousness was like. After Danny had dropped her home, she'd stripped off and collapsed into bed only to lay staring at the ceiling feeling bad for him.

Danny liked her, really liked her. It was in everything he did — the way he looked at her, cared for her, teased her and even bossed her around — and though she knew it was irrational, Beth had felt responsible for his obvious disappointment when he realised her stay in Levenham was only temporary.

What bothered her was that she felt disappointed too. Danny Burroughs was attractive, sweet, considerate and hard-working, all the things she could want in a man. But he was still a man who lived 1200 kilometres apart from her, in the wrong state, on the wrong side of the country.

He may as well have lived on the moon.

'Hey,' he said when she tried to brush past, his hand catching hers. 'What's up?'

Beth stood with her head down. What she wanted to do was bury her face in his strong chest and let him hold her and tell her everything would be okay. That she would survive the Christmas rush with all her orders done, her grandparents would return safely home with their business reputation intact, and that she and Danny would part friends and no one would have their heart broken.

'It's nothing. I'm just really, really tired.'

'I know you are.' He placed a finger under her chin and tipped it gently. His brown eyes were as warm and comforting as melted chocolate. 'That's why I'm here. To help you. I even brought my Santa hat for a bit of festive spirit.'

'Danny, you can't keep doing this. You have a life too.'

'Yeah, and I'll choose how I want to live it. And today I want to spend my time helping you. Now, how about some coffee?'

Beth wanted to argue but the truth was she wanted him here. Not only wanted but needed. Counting today, there were three shopping days remaining until Christmas and Beth had that many browband orders to complete, as well as Ebony's, and she would get Ebony's made even if she suffered permanent damage in the process. It would be her Christmas and thankyou present to Danny in one. There was nothing else she could offer.

'Coffee sounds good.' She smiled, her breath catching and her heart stuttering when Danny's gaze immediately dropped to her mouth and lingered there.

With perfect timing, the stereo switched to 'I Saw Mommy Kissing Santa Claus'. Danny's gaze shot back to Beth's and they both broke into laughter.

'You think the universe is telling us something?' he asked.

Before she could answer, the unmistakable chaos that is Christmas-hyped children erupted into the shop, followed by a weary order to behave from a mother well aware she had next to zero chance of being obeyed.

'Yes, that there's no rest for the wicked.'

And from the way Beth and Danny had been looking at one another, their thoughts had been veering toward very wicked indeed.

Fortunately, the mother had only ducked in to pick up some boots she'd had on order and was dealt with quickly. When Beth turned from the counter, Danny's cute mood had faded. His hands were on his hips and he had that bossy-boots look she was coming to associate with a reprimand.

'Have you had breakfast? And don't tell me you had a biscuit because there aren't any. There's no milk either and you're just about out of sugar.'

The fridge at her grandparents' house was equally bare. Along with cereal and bread, Beth had run out of milk days ago, and with no chance to grab groceries she'd been living on what she could scrounge from the cupboards, freezer, the shop and, more recently, Danny's generosity.

'I haven't exactly had a chance to shop, you know.'

'I'm taking that as a no. Right. I'll go get you something. What else do you need?'

'Danny . . .'

'Forget it. No time to argue, I'll figure it out.' And with that he strode off, leaving Beth gaping behind him.

Danny returned forty-five minutes later, laden with brand new green bags, his cheeks pink and an unusually flustered demeanour.

'There's fifteen thousand people in Levenham and I

swear every one of the buggers was at the supermarket this morning. Man, it was feral!'

'Did you have to buy bags?' The South Australian government had banned single-use plastic bags several years ago, forcing shoppers to carry reusable green bags with them all the time. Beth had been caught out herself when she'd first arrived and had grumbled at the inconvenience, but agreed the initiative was a good idea.

'Yeah. I usually have a couple in the ute for when I pick things up for Mum but I must have left them at home. Not to worry. Now you have shiny new ones.' He headed across the shop floor. 'You also have bread, cheese, ham, milk, eggs, fruit, biscuits, muesli bars, chocolate, sugar, more coffee pods, and a whole quiche from the bakery for breakfast.' He flashed her a grin. 'But we'll share that. I need it after the supermarket.'

Beth stood in the middle of the shop as he disappeared behind the counter and into the back, once again too flummoxed to speak.

She didn't know whether to be frustrated or grateful. He wasn't doing this because he wanted a Christmas present for his little sister, he was doing this for Beth, because he liked her and was trying to impress her. Like a gorilla beating its chest, or those birds that spent weeks building elaborate nests to attract a mate. Danny was showing her what a wonderful man he was, and he was. Truly wonderful.

But his investment was pointless. She was *leaving*. Why couldn't he see that?

Struck by a sudden urge to cry, Beth whirled to face the

window and the bright day outside. Traffic on the street was building. On the footpath in front of the charity shop, two women in sleeveless summer dresses stood chatting. A female jogger with a German shepherd on a leash sped past, then suddenly halted as she recognised the other women. The group hugged and kissed, and settled in for a natter in the sunshine.

Beth's teariness was replaced with longing for country town familiarity. She pressed her forehead against the glass and let its coolness seep into her skin. This wasn't for her. Danny wasn't for her. Beth had her life. She had a job and a flat, and her mum and Curtis close, and she was slowly making friends of her own. Other things would come in time.

'Beth?' Danny was standing at the workshop entrance. 'Come have some quiche while it's warm and it's quiet. You probably won't get a chance to eat later.'

Swallowing the roughness her longing had left in her throat, Beth nodded.

Danny waited for her at the counter, concern leaving thin crinkles at the corner of his eyes. 'You okay?'

'Uh huh.'

'Sure?'

She nodded, though Beth wasn't sure at all. His kindness was making her feel teary again.

He smiled and stroked a finger down the side of her face. 'You'll feel better once you have something to eat and some caffeine in your system.'

She breathed in deeply and let it out, and forced a smile.

'You're right. My blood sugar is probably zero right now.'

'Yep. Which is why I put three sugars in your coffee and two Tim Tams on your plate.'

While Sunday proved steady it was nothing like the previous days, but as Beth counted the takings it had still been worth opening. Usually the saddlery closed Saturday at lunchtime and didn't reopen until Monday, but Beth had put a notice on the door when she'd first arrived — well before she had any idea of the workload she'd be facing — that O'Brien's would be open every day until Christmas, and felt compelled to honour it.

Danny made himself invaluable. Having worked a till and credit card machine for years at the pub, learning the saddlery's system was a doddle. He was also friendly and well-known, and most customers seemed more than happy to deal with him. Unless her expertise was needed, Beth stayed in the workshop dealing with the last repairs and her browbands.

As with any profession historically dominated by men, a few people were unimpressed to be handed over to a woman when Danny called for assistance, continuing to address him as though he was the boss and expert and barely acknowledging Beth. A situation he dealt with quickly, and not without rebuke either. Beth had faced plenty of sexism in her career and was perfectly capable of handling it on her own, but Danny's defence still warmed her heart. It was nice to have someone on her side so fully. She didn't always get that in her current workplace.

When the takings were counted and reconciled, Beth deposited them in the safe and phoned her grandfather.

'How'd you fare today, Lizzy?' Grandpop had called her Lizzy from childhood and though it wasn't Beth's preferred shortening of her name, from his mouth it sounded like love.

'Good.' She rattled off the tally, and mentioned the couple of lay-bys that had been picked up. 'How's Grandma?'

'She's okay. Coming good. Barbara's fine too.'

'And you?'

'Itching to get home, Lizzy-love. What about yourself? You're sounding a bit tired. Everything all right? You eating okay? Still sleeping well in that old bed?'

'I'm going great, Grandpop. Eating and sleeping just fine.'

Danny looked up from the shelf he was tidying and raised an eyebrow. Beth poked her tongue out at him. He returned with a lazy grin followed by a blown kiss that made her heart do a long slow tumble-turn and her face to heat. She turned her back quickly and tried to focus.

'Have you sorted Christmas yet?' asked Grandpop.

'Not yet, but I'll be okay.' This year Beth planned to sleep Christmas Day away. And good riddance to it too.

'Lizzy-love, you can't spend Christmas alone. I tell you what, I'll give Audrey Wallace a tingle. Her grandchildren aren't much older than you and it's not like they don't have room in that ruddy great mansion of theirs. The Wallaces are good people, and young Emily's been riding all her life so you'll have plenty to talk about. They'd be thrilled to have you.'

'I'm fine, Grandpop, I promise.'

'Your grandma and I don't like the idea of you being alone. It's not right.'

She smiled at his concern. Her grandparents were such great people. Being dragged across the world only to be trapped within her parents' unhappiness and warring had made Beth's home life hard, but her grandparents remained constant. Always at the end of a phone, always promising help should Beth ever need it. She might not have experienced their love in person, and missed out on all the hugs and cuddles and beams of pride that other children had growing up, but she felt it all the same.

'I love you, Grandpop.'

Her grandfather coughed, as though embarrassed by the sudden affection. 'We love you too, Lizzy-love. Now, here, talk to your grandma. If she keeps jigging like that she'll bust her hip again.'

By the time Beth rang off, Danny had the shelves restocked and tidied, and the model horse wheeled inside, and was packing a green bag with the cold items from the fridge.

'You big fibber,' he said when she crouched to help.

'A white lie. I don't want them worrying.'

'You should have told them the truth.'

'What? That I'm about to collapse from exhaustion?'

'No, that you have a hunky Santa taking care of you.'

'Hunky?'

He nodded. 'Very hunky.'

'And not just a little bit conceited either.'

He stood with the bag and gathered up the rest of the morning's shopping. 'Right. Let's get this home, then you're coming for a drive.'

'A drive? No! I still have two browbands to finish.'

'Fireman's lift and a bum pat.' At her mutinous expression he added, 'Make that several bum pats.'

'Seriously, Danny, I can't.'

'Yes, Beth, you can.'

Beth should have known Danny would win. The argument had gone several more rounds but he was immovable. In the end it was easier to give in. Beth was too tired to fight anyway.

After dropping the groceries at her grandparents' house Danny drove west then took the main road south, past the extinct volcano that everyone local knew as Rocking Horse Hill, towards Port Andrews and the beach.

It had been years since Beth had been here, too long to remember with any clarity. As a little girl on visits from Adelaide, Grandpop and Grandma had brought her down to play in the sand, feed the seagulls and walk the breakwater, but those instances were more feelings now than real memories.

Her visit as a young teenager was clearer, and occurred on a rare trip to Australia with her mum. Dad hadn't come with them, citing work, but Beth knew it was really because he and Mum were in the middle of one of their silent wars. Later, those wars were no longer silent as they ceased all effort to hide their broken marriage from their daughter. At the time Beth had wondered if it was because they wanted her to hear. It wouldn't have surprised her. Her name seemed to crop up an awful lot in their fights.

She remembered the giant Norfolk Island pines that lined the esplanade, and the huge sweep of Admella Beach where surfers bounced the waves, and fisherman cast giant rods into gullies between the reefs where mulloway, whiting and bream were meant to bite. Mostly she remembered walking with Grandpop and Grandma, and feeling comforted from being with two people who cared for and loved each other, and treated each other with the kind of respect she never saw between her parents. It had almost made Beth ask if she could stay.

This evening the esplanade was busy with holiday makers, day trippers and locals out for a walk, and it took two laps before Danny scored a parking spot.

'What sort of fish do you like?' he asked as they walked towards a fish and chip shop that had surfboards and bikes leaning against its wall, and bare-chested youths lounging in colourful boardshorts on the tables outside.

'Whiting, if they have it. But I'll pay.'

'Nope.'

'Danny, be reasonable.'

'This is a date. I'm paying.'

Beth stopped on the footpath, almost causing the couple behind to crash into her. She apologised quickly before refocusing on Danny, who'd come to a halt a few steps on. 'A date?'

'Yes, a date.'

'Danny,' she said, exasperated. 'We can't be doing this.'

He stepped back close, his gaze molten and smiling. 'Yes, we can. It's Christmas.'

'What's Christmas got to do with it?'

'Everything.' He took her hand. 'Come on. I'm hungry, which means you're probably starving.'

She stumbled after him, still trying to get her head around his comment. A hundred questions and protests rattled her brain, but the chippie was crowded and rowdy and no place for discussion. A quick consultation of the board and Danny ordered and paid, shushing her protest with a finger to her mouth and another laughter-laden smile.

When their order was finally called, Danny carried their dinner to the foreshore and found a spot on the grass where they could dangle their legs over the side of the small sea wall separating the park from the sand and tide.

Though it wasn't even seven, daylight saving and their distance from the equator meant plenty of light remained. The sun sat huge against the crystalline sky and streaked the wave crests with gold. Beady-eyed seagulls hovered and squabbled at their feet, hungry for chips. The tide lapped the sand with hypnotic rhythm. It was vibrant, unpretentious, and a perfect first date setting.

They ate, hardly speaking, simply enjoying the beauty of the beach and the bustling village and the long summer day, and despite her confusion over Danny and her weary bones, Beth suddenly realised she felt happy.

'I needed this,' she said, popping a last chip in her mouth

before leaning back on her elbows to stare at the sea. 'I feel like I haven't seen daylight or smelled fresh air for weeks.'

'That's why I brought you here. Finished?'

At her nod, he gathered up the paper and scraps and took them to a nearby bin. On his return Beth expected him to sit close, but he kept an un-datelike distance between them and leaned on his elbows like her.

'This date business,' said Beth after a while. 'You know it won't lead anywhere.'

Danny slid a look her way, his mouth curved enigmatically. 'If you're talking about me hoping to get you into bed, I'm not that presumptuous. Not that I don't want to take you to bed, I do. Pretty damn badly. But I don't expect it.'

She rolled on her side and propped her head on her hand so she could study him properly. 'What *do* you expect?'

He copied her movement until they were facing one another, and reached to tangle his fingers with hers. 'I don't expect anything. What I'd *like* is to spend whatever time we have together, and I don't care how we do it.'

'But I'm leaving. My life is in Sydney.'

'I know, but you'll be back to visit.'

'Exactly. To visit. See, it's pointless.'

'Not pointless. Never pointless.'

'Then what is it?'

'What it is,' he said, leaning closer, his gaze flickering to her mouth, 'is right for now.' He paused as though considering the best way to kiss her, his breath light on her lips, his skin smelling of leather and lemon, of fish and chips and sunshine. 'Think of it as a little bit of Christmas magic.'

'Magic, huh?'

His mouth edged even closer, his voice low and husky. 'Well, yeah. I have been known to wear a Santa suit and channel the big fella on occasion.'

Everything inside Beth was fluttering. Pointless, stupid, whatever, she wanted this. She wanted *him*.

Her own voice dropped to a whisper. 'Your version is very naughty though.'

'Naughty but nice. Want me to show you?'

'Yes, please.'

It was all he needed. He caught her mouth with his, lips light, almost a brush. Then the brush developed purpose. Blood whooshing, Beth craned hungrily closer. Danny angled his head, accommodating her need, and with a soft groan the kiss went from ardent to fevered, the delicious joy of it shooting Beth's flutters winging into the sky.

With a prayer that their fall wouldn't be too hard, she let them go and gave into the thrill of Danny's touch.

Six

Oh, man. Not only did Beth look like his dream girl, she kissed like her too. Danny couldn't get enough. What was meant to be a short teasing kiss had turned so hot he had a hard-on like a flag pole. If he didn't pull away now he'd be in danger of doing something stupid, like sliding his hands up her top. Fine in private, not so fine on a very public beachfront with families picnicking and playing a few metres away.

He dragged his lips from her mouth and stared at her. She was flushed, her eyes hooded sexily, her breaths little pants. She looked like he felt — completely lust-ridden — and more gorgeous than ever.

'See?' he whispered, tracing her cheek with his finger, feeling awed. Danny had imagined a lot of things with Beth, but not this burst of emotion. Not this feeling of absolute rightness. 'Christmas magic.'

Beth blinked a few times before smiling. It was almost shy, as if she too had experienced something profound. 'Danny magic.'

'Not me. Us.'

The mention of 'us' had her expression clouding. She rolled onto her back and stared at the sky, top teeth on her bottom lip. 'This isn't going to end well, is it?'

He edged over to kiss her lightly. 'Stop thinking about the end. Enjoy the moment.'

Enjoy them falling in love because that's exactly what this was. Danny knew it and suspected Beth did too. She was just scared. He was as well, but Danny believed in something Beth had yet to realise — she belonged here. Beth might leave when her grandparents returned but she'd be back. He had plans to make damn sure of it.

She curled her soft hand around his jaw and studied his face. Then, ever so slowly, returned his smile. 'Okay. But only because it's Christmas.'

'Nothing to do with me being a hunky Santa?'

'Maybe a little,' she said, shifting her hand to his neck and drawing his head down to kiss him, before murmuring, 'Make that a lot,' and kissing him even harder.

In total contrast to Levenham Windmills — which was in Christmas wind-down with a skeleton staff and not much happening — the saddlery was chaos when Danny popped in Monday lunchtime bearing sandwiches, fruit and juice that he'd prepared at home early that morning. The queue at the counter was eight deep, with more shoppers browsing the racks.

Beth's hair was coming loose from her bun and there was

a dark oily smear across her red and white 'Team Santa' T-shirt. Her latest customer was umming and ahhing over her purchases, uncaring of the imaginary daggers she was being knifed with from those in line behind. Beth was trying to maintain her good humour, but for Danny — who'd experienced the glory of her genuine smiles and dreamed about earning more of them — her current brittle expression appeared in danger of morphing into a scream of pure frustration.

Danny didn't hesitate. He dumped their lunches out back, kissed Beth quickly on the cheek, and called up the next customer. Taking turns at the till, they dealt with the rest of the lunchtime rush until only the browsers remained. Beth took a weary step towards them but Danny stayed her arm.

'They'll be fine for a moment. Go eat.'

'What about you? Shouldn't you be back at work?'

Probably. He'd been here a while and his lunchbreak was likely well over, but not wanting Beth to feel guilty Danny ignored the urge to check. 'My work will be fine. Go and have your lunch. I can deal with the shop. Go!' he ordered when she hesitated. 'Or it'll be fireman's lift for you, missy.'

Beth threw up her hands. 'All right, all right.' But instead of leaving she eased up on tiptoe and kissed him. 'Thank you, hunky Santa.'

'The pleasure's all mine, gorgeous saddler girl.'

The flush that appeared on Beth's face kept Danny afloat for the rest of the afternoon. He arrived back at work thirty-five minutes late to a bit of ribbing from his boss, but didn't care. Beth had enjoyed a much-needed breather and lunch, and that's all that mattered. Thanks to his work ethic, Danny had accrued more than his share of brownie points over the years. A missed half-hour during Christmas wind-down was nothing.

He was worried about her though. With the shop so busy she'd have no opportunity to work on her orders. Tomorrow was Christmas Eve. Beth would have to labour into the night again to complete the remaining browbands and she'd already toiled past midnight last night on their return from Port Andrews. If it weren't for Danny threatening her with worse than fireman's lifts and forcing her home, he had no doubt she'd have kept slogging until she collapsed.

To make matters worse, Danny had shifts at the pub for the next two nights and wouldn't be on hand to keep an eye on her. Extreme tiredness had the same effect on the human body as drunkenness, and with all the sharp tools Beth used she was at real risk of injury.

The thought made Danny jittery, but cancelling his shifts was out of the question. Another time of the year he might have gotten away with it but not at Christmas. All he could do was call when he had the chance, and hope like hell she'd stay safe until he turned up to take her home.

'You have to stop, Beth. Right now.'

'I can't!' She was almost wailing with frustration but Danny didn't care. There were dark circles under her eyes and her fingers were trembling from too much caffeine, fatigue, cramp, or all three. 'They're coming in the morning to pick it up. You saw the shop today. If I don't get it done now it'll never be finished.'

'It's one o'clock. You're dead on your feet. Stuff the frigging browband.' Danny placed his hands on the work bench and loomed over her. He needed to win this fight for Beth's sake, although it was hard to look authoritative and macho in a Santa suit. 'We're finishing up at lunch tomorrow. I'll come straight from work and man the shop for you, and you can work on it in the afternoon.'

'They're coming in the morning!'

'Phone them first thing and tell them it won't be ready until later.'

'I can't! They're leaving for Bendigo after lunch. It has to be finished tonight.' Beth's eyes turned bright with tears. 'I know you're trying to look after me but I've already put them off once. It's for their granddaughter. I can't let them down.'

Danny quit looming and gently cupped her face instead. 'I just hate seeing you like this.'

Beth gave a choked, humourless laugh. 'You mean all stressed and teary and ugly?'

'Never ugly. You're beautiful all the time.'

'Liar. I look awful.'

'Not to me.'

Her smile was tired and watery, but still a smile, and Danny loved her for battling against the weight of the pressure she was under.

'You have all the lines,' she said.

'Not lines, truth.' He kissed her and let her go. 'Okay. Keep working, but one wrong move and it'll be fireman's lift, okay?'

Danny settled back on his stool to watch Beth with hawk eyes. At least the rosettes were made and she was up to stitching them to the nylon strip. It was tight work though and she had to pause every few minutes to stretch the cramp from her fingers. He couldn't wait for Christmas day when this would be over for her.

Christmas Day. Danny wished he could spend all of it with Beth, but as usual the extended Burroughs clan was descending on the farm, and Beth probably had an aunt or cousin or something she'd booked in with. Danny wondered if he knew them.

'So who has the pleasure of your gorgeous company this Christmas lunch?'

'No one.'

'What do you mean no one? Aren't you going to a relative's or something?'

'There's no one really here. A couple of cousins I think, but I don't know them.' Beth picked up a blue-and-red rosette and dabbed a spot of glue on its base. 'I have one plan for Christmas Day and that's to sleep it away.'

'Not any bloody more you don't. You're coming home with me.'

She set down the needle she'd just picked up. 'Danny . . .'

'No. Don't even think of arguing. I don't care how tired you are, you can't sleep all day, and I refuse to spend my Christmas day fretting about you being alone when you've a perfectly normal family who'd love to have you.'

'You can't just invite a stranger out for Christmas lunch.'

'You're not a stranger. You know Mum and Ebs, and you know me. Besides, there's seventeen adults and I can't remember how many kids coming for lunch. One more's hardly going to make a dent. I'll pick you up at ten thirty so you'll have plenty of time to sleep in, and if you feel tired after lunch you can either collapse in my room for a while or I'll bring you back.'

Danny stood to pace, excited by the idea. Christmas with Beth and his family. It was like, well, Christmas.

'You wait,' he said, 'it'll be great. We can take a couple of quads for a spin around the farm and Ebs will want to show you Hobbles and all her horse stuff. Nick'll be jealous and probably try to steal you off me and we'll have to have a manly wrestle to prove who's strongest. Which will be me, of course.'

Beth laughed. 'Of course.'

'There'll be more food than anyone can eat and kids running around hyper, and everyone looking stupid in paper hats and laughing at the cracker jokes even though they're shocking.' He stopped in front of her. 'Christmas magic, Beth.'

'Certainly sounds that way.'

'Good. Then we're set.'

'Assuming I haven't gone mad in between times.' She set down the rosettes and regarded them with hunched shoulders. 'I'm sorry, Danny. I haven't even started on Ebony's browband.'

In a heartbeat he was crouching beside her and holding her close, kissing her hair and face and rubbing soothing hands over her back. 'Don't you dare feel bad about that. Ebs will be fine. I'll pick out something else.'

'But—'

'No. No more, Beth. This is the last one.' He pulled back so he could look her in the eye. 'Okay?'

Her mouth remained closed and her chin lifted a fraction. Defiance flashed in her hazel eyes.

'I know what you're thinking and you can stop right now. When the shop closes tomorrow night, that's it.'

'I want to do this.'

'I don't care. No more. You need rest and I'm not having you work yourself to exhaustion for me.' He kissed her. 'Promise me you'll let it go.'

'No.'

Danny pressed his forehead against hers and turned his voice low and gruff. 'Yes.'

'No,' she said, sounding slightly like an obstinate toddler, which was cute but frustrating. 'Not going to. Now, if you've quite finished being a bossy boots, I have work to do.'

Seven

At the sound of the shop door opening, Beth shoved the pink-and-blue rosette she was working on under a square of plain leather and dashed for the counter. It was nearing lunchtime and Danny had promised he'd be in straight after knock-off. Christmas Eve morning had so far proved a let-down takings-wise but a boon for Beth work-wise. Between her early start and lack of customers, she'd managed almost five rosettes for Ebony's browband, but it was progress she didn't want Danny spotting in case he guessed her plan.

He was striding across the shop towards her looking ridiculously capable and handsome in a pair of light khaki cargo-style work trousers and matching shirt. 'Hey, gorgeous saddler girl.'

Beth smiled and held her face up for a kiss. 'Hello, manly tradie person.'

'Manly tradie person, huh?' He brushed his mouth against hers once, then again, and, with a rapid glance around the shop and flash of wicked grin, settled in for a long, lingering kiss that turned Beth liquid and breathless with want. 'I like the sound of that.'

'Funny. I couldn't tell.' She poked him playfully in the chest. 'You're early.'

'Boss decided to let us go. Reckons I was useless anyway. Too busy thinking about you.' He stroked her face then peered toward the empty car park. 'I thought you'd be flat out but it's dead.'

'There's been a few people in, but mostly it's been really quiet. I guess the majority have finished their gift shopping.'

'Might pick up this afternoon.'

'I feel awful for saying this but I hope not.' On cue a yawn formed. After covering her mouth, Beth stretched her arms towards the ceiling and arched her back, groaning softly as her stiff muscles protested.

Danny's gaze shot to her chest, his grin turning sheepish when she caught the intensity of his stare. 'Sorry. Man habit.' He leaned close, his hand on Beth's waist where her Rudolf the Red-Nosed Reindeer T-shirt had ridden up, his work-roughened fingers shooting tingles across her skin. 'Can't blame me. They're pretty fantastic.'

Beth wanted to laugh but was too distracted by the slide of his fingers and the way his thumb was caressing circles over her hip. With every stroke, the aches faded until there was nothing but the pure energy of desire remaining.

He nuzzled her neck. 'You're so soft. I don't want to stop touching you.'

'You have to.' If he didn't she'd combust. Or melt. Or flip the 'Open' sign on the shop door to 'Closed', drag him out the back and strip those oh-so-sexy work clothes off that lean, muscled body and kiss it all over.

Danny stopped stroking and rested his face against the hollow of her collarbone for a few breaths, before taking a step back and shoving his hand though his hair. 'Sorry. That kind of just happened. So,' he said, plunging his fists into his pockets and resting his bum against the counter, 'have they been in?'

Beth blinked at him. Lust had fuddled her brain and she had no idea who he meant. 'Who?'

'The browband people.'

'Oh.' She pressed the heel of her hand to her left eyebrow where a persistent headache had been throbbing most of the morning, until Danny's kiss banished it. The mention of browbands made it pulse again. 'Yes, about an hour ago. They were thrilled.'

'I should bloody well hope so after the hours you put in.'

Beth couldn't agree more, but she couldn't complain when the whole mess had been her own fault. Taking on so many orders had been silly but they were done now — the paid-for ones, at least — and the relief was unbelievable. Danny had turned up at the saddlery after his pub shift last night and found Beth almost manic with it. She'd knotted off the final stitch only five minutes before and the joy of finishing had seen her racing to the door and launching into his arms. Realising what it meant, Danny had twirled her around in celebration, and when Beth dragged him over to look, he'd dutifully inspected her work.

'It looks perfect,' he'd said. 'You know what this means, don't you?'

'A kiss from the big red man?'

He'd laughed and obliged. 'You can have a kiss anytime. Nope, what this means is bed.'

Beth's eyebrows had shot up. 'Aren't you a saucy Santa?'

'I wish. No, my gorgeous, talented Beth, there'll be no saucy Santa-ing tonight. You're going to bed alone and straight to sleep, even if I have to sit by your side and sing you lullabies all night.'

After helping her lock up, Danny had driven her home and walked her to the porch. 'It's over now,' he'd said, kissing her tenderly. 'No more browbands. No more stress. Just rest.'

'So you say,' Beth had murmured, then tried to distract him with a kiss. But her tone had Danny pulling away to regard her with narrowed eyes. Clearly her expression had lacked innocence.

'Don't even think it.'

'No harm in thinking.'

'Beth . . .' His gaze narrowed even further. 'I warned you.'

'You did.' She smiled sweetly. 'But I never said I'd obey.'

Danny had made a growling noise that made her giggle and him growl even more. The macho act fooled no one. He could growl and act as bossy as he liked, but behind that Santa suit Danny was a big softie.

'Shh,' she'd said, resting a finger on his lips. 'You'll upset the neighbour's dogs.'

'Beth, if you get sick . . .'

'I won't. Now,' she tapped his lips, 'don't you think you'd better get home too? You have work tomorrow.' As much as Beth adored his protectiveness, with the early start she had planned Beth needed sleep. So did Danny.

He cradled her face and regarded her worriedly. 'Promise me you'll rest.'

'I will. I promise.' Just not for as long as Danny wanted.

He'd searched her face for several beats longer, then with a final sigh and lingering kiss had left, tossing suspicious looks over his shoulder as he walked the path. With justification. Though Beth was rubbery with fatigue, she'd brushed her teeth, set her alarm for five thirty and, too tired to put on her shortie pyjamas, had crawled into bed naked. The alarm, then a shower and a bowl of cereal roused her back to life, and by six-fifteen she was at her workbench, dosing on double strength coffee and cutting out pink and blue leather petals for Ebony's browband.

At her workbench was where Beth planned to spend Christmas Eve too, after Danny had gone to work. It'd take some sneaking, perhaps even a small fib or two that she'd feel guilty about, but the end would be worth it.

'What do you want for lunch?' asked Danny, bringing Beth back to the present. 'Seeing as it's quiet I could duck home and bring us back a couple of sandwiches. Or I could raid the bakery. Maybe grab us a couple of pies.'

'Sandwiches sound perfect.' And would give her another window of work time. With still so much to do, every minute counted.

'Anything else?'

Beth shook her head. 'I brought fruit and juice from home.'

Danny gave the car park a final inspection but the only vehicle was his ute. 'You sure you'll be okay?'

'More than okay.'

'All right. Don't do anything silly while I'm gone.'

'Like what?'

'I dunno, fall for some random bloke in a Santa suit.'

'Not a chance,' said Beth, curling her arms around his neck for a kiss. 'The one I have is perfect already.'

She followed him to the door, enjoying the weight of his arm around her shoulders, and stayed watching until his ute turned on to the road. The moment it disappeared she raced back to her bench. With a bit of luck, Beth would fit in one more rosette during his absence.

The saddlery did pick up in the afternoon, but in comparison to other days it was an easy run. Unable to work on Ebony's browband with Danny present, Beth took the chance to give the saddlery a good tidy. The shop would be closed Christmas and Boxing Day, reopening Friday and Saturday morning, and it would be nice to come in to find it clean and the shelves stacked.

'I need to pick out something for Ebs,' said Danny, when they'd finally run out of chores. 'Any thoughts?'

'Not really,' said Beth. 'I don't know what she has.'

Danny's nose screwed up. 'Everything. That pony has more leather gear than a BDSM parlour.'

'What about clothes then?'

'Same. Mum bought her a new riding jacket at the start of the show season. And jodhs.'

'Boots?'

'Got 'em.'

Beth chewed her lip, debating whether to tell him about the browband. 'What about a book or a video?'

'Knowing Ebs, she probably has them all.' Danny let out a huff. 'Maybe I should shoot up the street and buy her a voucher from that dress shop she likes.'

'Or from here. We do vouchers.'

'That's it, then. That way she can't blame me for buying the wrong thing.'

It was a compromise, certainly, but a voucher wasn't very personal and Beth could tell from Danny's air of gloom he felt bad about resorting to one. Though he'd made jokes about how annoying Ebony was, they were said with love. Danny adored his little sister. He adored his whole family. That fierce love and loyalty were just two of the many things Beth admired about him.

'What about . . .' She bent behind the glass display counter where Grandpop kept small, valuable items like equine-inspired jewellery, collectables and the like. Beth scanned the contents, searching for something nice but inexpensive, and settled on a gold-plated tie-pin in the shape of a hunting crop with a horseshoe at its centre. She set it on the counter and slid it towards Danny.

He scratched his jaw. 'I don't know. It's a bit old for her, maybe.' He crouched on the opposite side and pointed to a box containing a necklace and pair of coloured enamel and silver earrings in the shape of a prancing horse. 'What about those?'

They were dear. Much dearer than the price of the browband. Beth didn't want him spending more than necessary, if she could help it. A cheaper silver bracelet sat alongside the box but it was still too much. The bracelet gave her an idea though. She chewed her lip, thinking, then checked the clock. It was after four. Not much time, but if Danny was quick she could get it done before his shift at six.

'I have an idea, but we'll need to hurry if you're to make your shift on time.'

'Hit me.'

'A bracelet made of plaited leather with strands from her pony's tail woven inside. I can also knot one of those silver charms to the end to make it a bit prettier. It'll take me no time to do. It's the time to get the horse hair that's tight.'

Danny was around the counter before she'd finished speaking, his hands cupping her face. 'You're not only gorgeous, you're a genius.' He kissed her hard. 'How much hair do you need?'

'Not much. A dozen strands, maybe a few more.'

With another kiss he was gone. Forty minutes later he was back, red-faced but grinning, and with several long black horsetail hairs curled in an envelope.

'That was hairy,' he said, handing the envelope over and following Beth into the workshop where she'd already laid out four long thin leather thongs. 'And I don't mean Hobbles' tail. Mum pulled in with Ebs just as I'd finished snipping. Ebs was out of the car like a shot demanding to know what I was doing. Had to make up some excuse about seeing a bot fly and wanting to cut off any eggs it might have laid straight away. I don't think she believed me.'

Beth carefully smoothed the hairs alongside the outer leather strip. 'She'll understand tomorrow.'

She considered for a moment and lifted the hairs aside. 'I think I'll plait the tail hair first then add them in. It's more work and a bit fiddly but should help make the bracelet more durable. Otherwise the strands might work loose from the leather and catch and break.'

By the time Beth finished plaiting the hair her hands were aching. She shook away the pain and aligned the plaited strand with the outside leather thong. Satisfied, she knotted the leather and hair lengths together and pinned the knot to the bench. With a last alignment and loosening hand shake, she began to weave.

Danny pulled up a stool and watched her work. 'You're so fast.'

'It's easy. Most girls have been plaiting hair since they were little.'

'Yeah, but that has four strands, not three.'

'Same principle, just a bit more concentration. If I had more time and more hair, I could have done a herringbone plait with eight strands, a bit like what you do with whips. They look lovely.' She wove a little more, taking care to keep the tension even. 'I used to make leather bracelets and necklaces as gifts for my friends back home. All sorts of styles, depending on what suited best.'

'You must miss them. Your friends, I mean.'

'I do, but there are plenty of ways to keep in touch, and I'm making new ones.' She slanted him a look. 'Some happen to be *very* friendly.'

Danny's return look was equally suggestive. 'I can be friendlier.'

'I'm sure.'

After several pauses to shake the cramp from her hands, and a short break to select a suitable charm from the cabinet, the plaiting was complete. Beth wove and back-spliced one end into a loop and used a metal clamp to lock the plait and loop in place. The other end she also clamped, then trimmed the hair but left the thongs long and loose so they could be threaded through the loop and knotted to secure the bracelet.

'Done,' she said, presenting it to Danny.

He fingered the work, his expression awed and proud. 'You're amazing.'

'Not really. It was easy.'

'I don't care. To me you're amazing.' He gathered her to him. 'Amazing, gorgeous, fun, talented, beautiful. No wonder I'm crazy about you.' Danny nuzzled her ear, shooting electric shocks up and down Beth's spine. His voice lowered to a husky, seductive whisper. 'Did I mention you also have great breasts?'

She giggled into his shirt and wrapped her arms around him. Cuddling Danny was like cuddling home. When the time came, Beth didn't know how she was going to leave, but she supposed it would be like her friends in England — they'd find ways keep in touch.

Except you couldn't put your arms around a phone call, email, text or instant message. You couldn't kiss them, couldn't adore them. No matter the words, no matter the image, none would ever come close to the way Danny made her feel: loved.

Eight

Beth had only just guided her wobbly legs towards the shower and stripped off when the doorbell chimed. Still groggy with sleep, she screwed her nose up at the noise. Surely it was too early for visitors? Whoever it was could go away. Until she showered and washed last night's fatigue and sleep from her eyes and body, Beth wouldn't be in any state to greet anyone.

The doorbell chimed again.

And again.

With a groan, she tugged her towel off the bathroom rail and staggered to the lounge with it held against her chest. Easing back the curtain, she squinted outside. Christmas Day blazed with too-bright brilliance and it took several blinks for her grit-filled eyes to adjust. Catching sight of the person standing on her grandparents' porch, her frown turned even deeper. It couldn't be . . . but it was, which meant either Danny was eager-early or she'd overslept badly.

A quick check of the mantel clock revealed how badly.

Beth took an indulgent moment to bang her head softly against the window pane and groan. Then, pathetic, poor-me moment over, she stepped away from the window, wrapped the towel tight around her naked body and lumbered to the door.

'Sorry, sorry, sorry,' she wailed as she flung it open.

Danny's face registered surprise, followed quickly by something else entirely when he saw what she was — or wasn't — wearing. His gaze swept lazily over her body before landing, sparkly with amusement, on her face. 'Now there's a Christmas present I'd like to unwrap.'

'I'm so sorry. Mum rang early to wish me merry Christmas, and seeing I was awake I called Grandpop and Grandma and Aunty Barbara to do the same for them, but it was only eight thirty so I went back to bed thinking I'd sneak in another hour, and didn't bother with the alarm because I thought I'd wake in plenty of time, but I fell straight back to sleep and—'

'Shush,' he said, stepping inside and cupping her face. 'You're fine. I'm glad you slept in. You needed it. By the way, merry Christmas.'

Then he kissed her with an intensity that burst starlight through her fuddled brain and had Beth contemplating stripping off her towel and dragging him to bed.

'Merry Christmas to you too,' she replied breathlessly when Danny finally let her go. Realising the towel had loosened she tugged at the edge to tighten it, which only attracted Danny's attention. From his height, he could peer right between her breasts. The curve of his mouth indicated how much he appreciated the view.

'No need for modesty on my account,' he said, not bothering to shift his focus.

'My face is up here, you know.'

'I know. But your boobs are down there.' He shook his head in admiration. 'God's gift to man.'

Beth giggled, and with it the panic of running horrendously late subsided. 'Come in. You can wait in the kitchen while I shower. The kettle's there if you want a cuppa or there's some of that juice you bought in the fridge. Turn the telly on, if you want.'

'I'd much rather watch you shower.'

Beth would too, but if they started down that path they'd never make it back to Danny's farm and Beth had a special present to deliver.

She left Danny to amuse himself and bathed as fast as she could but it still seemed to take forever. Beth had been too busy to take care of herself lately and there was hair to wash and dry, plus some in dire need of removal, body lotion to rub in and a light layer of makeup to apply. Though she'd met Ebony and Judy Burroughs before, today she was meeting the whole family and Beth very much wanted to look pretty and nice for Danny.

'Ta da!' she said, waltzing into the kitchen and doing a twirl.

For a long moment Danny stared without speaking, then he made a moaning noise and ran his hand through his hair. 'Oh, man.'

Beth stiffened. 'Is it wrong?'

She tugged at the hem of her dress. It was a simple button through white dress printed with small blue flowers, with cap sleeves, a sweetheart neckline and fitted waist. Skimming a respectable four inches above her knees it was cute and summery and, she'd erroneously believed, ideal for a hot Australian Christmas lunch.

'It's too short, isn't it? I'll go change. I have some shorts that should do. It's just that I thought a dress would be nice and I only packed one.'

She turned to walk to her room but Danny caught her hand and whipped her back into his arms. 'The dress is perfect.' His gaze raked her hair, for once long and loose and flyaway from being freshly washed and blow-dried. 'Your hair is perfect.' He stroked it almost reverentially before dipping his gaze to her mouth, shiny with pale pink lip gloss. 'Your mouth is perfect. *You* are perfect.'

'So what's the matter?'

'How the hell am I meant to keep my hands off you?'

Relief had Beth breathing again. 'Ever heard of self-control?'

'Even superheroes have their weaknesses, and that dress is kryptonite.'

'I'm sure you'll manage.'

'I'm bloody sure I won't.' He stared at her mouth. 'You are so kissable right now.'

'As opposed to?'

'I'm not sure it'd be smart to reveal what I'm thinking the other times.'

Beth's laugh was cut short by Danny's mouth closing over

hers. It was a kiss filled with promise, heat and anticipation, and left them with their foreheads pressed together, sharing a smile as they stared in wonder at each other.

'You taste like berries,' he said.

'It's the gloss.'

'I don't think there's any left on.'

'That's okay. I have more.'

'Good, because I want more.'

'So do I,' whispered Beth, and they both knew she wasn't talking about the gloss. She didn't want to break the connection but it was Christmas Day and Beth had already made them late. She slid her arms from his neck and tugged at his shirt. 'Your family must be wondering where you are.'

'Probably.'

'Well?'

Danny sighed and reluctantly released his grip.

She patted his chest in sympathy and crossed to the back door where her elastic-sided leather boots were arranged on a rack. She picked them up. 'Shall I throw these in?' She was wearing sandals but if Danny planned on taking her on a tour of the farm, she'd need boots.

'Good idea.'

He took them from her, leaving Beth free to collect her tote-bag. When Danny tried to carry that too she shook her head and hooked the straps over her shoulder. Snuggled at the bottom of the bag, wrapped in tissue paper she'd scrounged from Grandma's sewing room late last night, was Ebony's browband. Having him discover it now would only cause trouble.

'Should I bring anything else?' asked Beth.

'Maybe a hat, but if you don't have one there's plenty at the farm.'

With everything gathered, Beth snatched up her keys and followed Danny to the door, admiring his bum as he walked. He was looking delicious himself in neat camel shorts and a chambray shirt with the sleeves rolled up, deck shoes and a matching belt. When he paused to open the front door, Beth slipped her hand over his rear and gave it a teasing squeeze.

'Ever heard of self-control?' he asked.

'I probably won't get to touch you again for a while.'

'Don't worry, I'll find a way.' He bent to kiss her gently, stroking her cheek with one finger as his lips lingered and his voice dropped deep and low. 'With you I'll always find a way.'

His words had Beth's heart fluttering.

She fumbled the keys twice while locking the door, not least because Danny was standing close behind her, one hand lazily tracing up and down her waist while skipping whisper soft kisses along her collarbone.

'You have to stop that.'

'You started it, bum fondler.'

He had a point.

'Did Ebony like her bracelet?' asked Beth as they strapped themselves into Danny's ute.

'Loved it.'

'She wasn't disappointed about the browband?'

His hesitation gave Beth the answer. She'd made the right decision in sneaking back to the shop last night to finish Ebony's present after Danny dropped her home, even if she had sent herself cross-eyed working until two thirty in the morning to complete it.

'She understood.' He steered the ute away from the kerb and headed to the corner. 'The bracelet made up for it. She was rapt with that. Hasn't stopped showing it off.'

'That's lovely.' Beth pointed out the windscreen. 'Eyes on the road, Santa-man.'

Danny grinned and reached across to lay his warm palm on her bare thigh. 'I'll look with my hands then.'

Beth had expected the roads to be quiet but there were cars travelling in to and out of town. People out visiting or heading for lunches, she supposed. From the main highway west, Danny turned right onto a narrow bitumen road. Beth studied the landscape with interest.

'The soils around here are mostly volcanic from Mount Pitt,' said Danny. 'Everyone knows Rocking Horse Hill because it still looks like a volcano. Mount Pitt is more an eroded mound, but we're still proud of it. Our place is on the Levenham side, surrounded by dairy farms. We gave that up years ago but my Uncle Des still milks. His place it to the north-west of us, and we also have cousins with dairy farms to the south.' Danny grinned. 'Mount Pitt is packed with Burroughs. You should see the sports centre. We're all over the honour boards.'

'What do you do on your farm if not dairy?'

'Hay, silage, beef. We also contract finish heifers for a few dairy farms.' He noticed her incomprehension. 'Basically that means taking weaners and looking after them until their first mating. Some farmers don't have, or don't want to spare the land to raise their heifers, but if you don't look after them properly you can end up with calving problems and lower milk production down the track. That's where we can help.'

Beth noted the ongoing use of 'we' and the pride in his voice and expression. 'You sound as though you're pretty involved.'

'Nah. The farm's Nick and Dad's domain. I have my own job.'

'But you still love it.'

'I do, but not as much as I like tooling around with metal.' He sneaked his hand a little further up her thigh. 'Or other things.'

'Remember that black thing in front of us?' said Beth, pushing his hand towards her knee. 'It's called a road. You're meant to keep your eyes on it.'

Danny's grin was unrepentant.

The paddocks were a vast mosaic of irrigated greenery and hayed-off blonde. Herds of Friesians with pendulous udders strip-grazed lush electric-fenced pastures, while other paddocks held red and white beef cattle and the occasional black one. All the livestock were muscled and full-bellied, and glossy with good health, the pastures verdant and thick. A fairy-tale farmland, and more than a little like home.

'It reminds me of where I grew up,' she said, stroking the window with a curled finger. 'Kent is like that. Green everywhere.'

Danny patted her knee. 'You should feel right at home then.'

Strangely, she did, even if the Christmas weather was totally topsy-turvy. She wondered if her dad would have a white Christmas this year. Beth guessed she'd find out when he called her later.

'Everyone's really excited that you're coming. Ebs especially.'

'My grandparents are too. They were worried I was going to spend Christmas alone, although they were very curious about how I managed to be invited.'

'What did you tell them?'

'Not much.' She slid him a sideways look. 'Only that I was seduced by Santa, and that he's champion snogger.'

Danny made a choking noise then laughed. 'Thanks. You're not too bad yourself.' He was quiet a moment. 'You're the first girlfriend I've ever spent Christmas with.'

'Same here.'

'Good. I like that. Makes it more special for the both of us.'

'Don't count your chickens,' Beth said seriously, but inside she was full of warm fuzziness. The way Danny deemed everything they did together as special was very sweet. 'It could all end in disaster.'

'I don't think so.' He took his eyes off the road to check her face. She kept her expression sombre to foil him. 'Okay, how?'

'Oh, I could get drunk, slop food over myself, and then run off with your brother.'

'No, you wouldn't. Nick's an idiot and I'm smarter and better looking.'

'If you do say so yourself.'

'I do. I've known it from birth.'

'Conceited.'

'Crazy about you.' He smiled and curled his hand in hers and squeezed. 'Christmas magic, Beth. That's what we'll be making today, Christmas magic. You just wait.' Danny glanced at the road and his expression took on a keen edge. He pointed ahead. 'That fence marks the start of our place.'

Beth leaned forward, studying the paddocks closely. Letting go of her hand, Danny slipped his under her hair and smoothed the back of her neck.

'How big is it?'

'Eighteen hundred acres. Most of it's pretty intensively farmed. Plenty to keep Dad and Nick busy. When hay season's in full swing both Mum and I help out, Ebs too. And Pops, of course.'

'A real family affair.'

'Yeah, it's good. See that?' Danny pointed to a shiny galvanised windmill.

'One of yours?'

'Yep.'

Beth smiled. She bet he wore that same satisfied look each time he spotted a Levenham Windmill, and his pride made her feel a bit wistful. What did Beth have to feel like that about? Except for probably Ebony's, she'd never see her browbands on the horses and ponies they were made for. In her current job she rarely made it out of the workshop, whereas Grandpop in his heyday made a point of visiting shows and local horse events to talk to owners about their purchases, fit saddles, and trend spot.

These days her grandparents had eased back, preferring to take weekends off to relax. Perhaps with retirement in their sights and the sale of the saddlery the most likely future, they saw no point. The thought stabbed sadness through Beth's chest. The saddlery had been her grandparents' life and although Beth had spent little time there, it mattered to her because it mattered to them. Losing it would hurt.

She glanced at Danny, so handsome and happy and sure of himself. So unashamed or scared of what was happening between them. Yes, losing O'Brien's would hurt, but Beth knew from the way her heart somersaulted and swelled at his smile, his touch, his affection, that losing Danny would hurt even more.

And with every moment they spent together, the further she fell, that pain would only get worse.

'We're here,' said Danny, slowing the ute and indicating. He glanced at her, his smile wide and lit with excitement. 'Ready?'

Remembering Danny's counsel to stop thinking about the end and enjoy the moment, Beth took a deep breath and nodded. It was Christmas. Not just any Christmas, but Christmas with Danny and the family he adored.

Whatever happened in the future, today would be worth it.

Nine

The Burroughs' kitchen was redolent with the aroma of roasting meat and the spicy scent of pudding. Judy greeted Beth with a delighted hug and kiss on the cheek, before introducing her to the other women and children crowding the kitchen, along with an order not to worry if she couldn't remember their names — most of the family couldn't keep up either. There were aunts and cousins and nieces and nephews, plus Danny's two grandmothers, both of whom eyed Beth with beady curiosity.

'Be nice, you two,' said Danny, kissing them each on the cheek. 'No scaring my girlfriend away. I want to keep this one.'

It was the second time Danny had called her his girlfriend. The first time, in the car, Beth hadn't thought anything of it because it was in a private moment, but this time she raised an eyebrow. Danny wasn't remotely chastened. He simply grinned and shrugged, as if to say, 'well, you are', while his grandmothers observed the exchange with interest.

Introductions made, Danny took her hand and indicated a wide doorway at the other end of the kitchen. 'Ebs and the rest are keeping out of trouble in here.'

The door opened into a large lounge. Ebony was in one corner, sitting cross-legged next to a Christmas tree with a book open on her lap, and surrounded by crumpled and torn wrapping paper. Four men were at the other end of the lounge, watching a remote-controlled monster truck perform wheelies on the carpet. Although his hair was longer and scruffier, from his age and likeness to Danny, Beth guessed the man with the remote was Nick.

'Beth's here,' announced Danny, with pride in his voice.

Nick's head whipped up. For a few heartbeats he stared at Beth's face with what seemed to be astonishment, before lowering his gaze and subjecting her to an indulgent up and down that had Danny tugging her closer and glaring at his brother.

Formal introductions were interrupted by first the truck crashing into the chair, then Ebony flinging herself at Beth with a squeal.

'Nicholas Burroughs, what did I tell you?' Judy stalked across the room and snatched up the truck and dumped it into her son's arms. She jerked a thumb at the window. 'You want to play like a six year old, you do it outside. Got it?'

'Yes, Mum.'

Danny's scowl turned into a grin. Nick surreptitiously flipped him the bird, then deliberately gave Beth another flirty once-over. It was so obviously designed to annoy Danny that Beth felt an urge to present him with her own middle finger.

'Thanks so, so much for the bracelet,' said Ebony, releasing Beth from her bear hug and raising her wrist to show the bracelet circling it. The young girl's excited face glittered brighter than the Christmas tree. 'It's the best thing. The best!'

'Better than a browband?' said Beth teasingly and immediately regretted it when she saw the confusion on Ebony's face. Realising the poor girl didn't know how to answer without causing offence, she rushed on. 'Just as well you don't have to choose then.'

Beth rummaged in her tote bag, extracted the tissue-wrapped gift and held it out.

Ebony's mouth popped open like a sideshow alley clown. Wide-eyed, she looked from it, to Beth, to Danny, and back to the paper.

Beth nodded. 'Go on.'

Ebony regarded the gift as though it were preciously fragile. Then her astonishment broke to an ecstatic grin and she tore off the tissue paper with puppy-like eagerness. For a few seconds she stared, her chest rising and falling as though she'd run a mile, finger reverently tracing the tiny pink and blue rosettes.

'Oh,' she said. 'Oh!' Then with another squeal wrapped her arms around Beth's waist and hugged her. 'Thank you, thank you, thank you!'

Over the moon to have brought so much joy, Beth hugged her back. Ebony's delight had made the late nights and hard work worth it. She turned to smile at Danny only for her heart to stutter at the disbelief in his expression. Swallowing, Beth looked away. She glanced at Judy and the men to see if they'd noticed, but everyone's focus was on Ebony.

With a wriggly kind of foot-stomping dance, Ebony let Beth go. 'I have to show Hobbles!' And with that she dashed off, browband held aloft like an Olympic torch.

'Well done,' said Nick, approaching with his hand held out. 'I'm Nick, the brother you should have chosen.'

Beth shook, flushing a little at his jibe and lingering handshake.

'Cut it, Numbnuts,' growled Danny, draping an arm around Beth's shoulders.

Nick merely grinned, only for it to vanish when one of the approaching men clipped him over the ear.

'Behave yourself,' the older man ordered, then he presented Beth with a smile so broad it made the crow's feet around his eyes fan almost to his temples. 'Welcome to the madhouse. I'm Steve, Danny's dad. This is my brother Des and my cousin Michael.'

Beth shook hands with each of them, every grip confident, every smile genuine and it was easy to see where Danny got his good nature from, as well as his athletic build. The Burroughs were an attractive family, in more ways than looks.

'Happens we all went to school with your mum,' said Steve. 'Des and I weren't in the same year but young Michael here was. Pretty girl. You look a lot like her. How is Ang these days? Be donkeys since I last saw her.'

'Really well. She lives in Sydney now with her new partner and works part-time for a local library, which suits Mum because she loves to read.'

'And you're a saddler, like your grandfather. I bet that makes him proud.'

'I hope so.'

Danny's arm stayed around Beth as she continued to chat, but she could feel the tension in his muscles. Beth wasn't sure if it was because of the browband or Nick's continued efforts to wind him up.

At the first break in conversation, Danny excused them. Cupping her elbow, he steered Beth down a hall and into a room midway along, closing the door behind them. Beth leaned against the wall and scanned the room. It was neat and masculine, with a queen-sized bed topped with a plain blue and black doona. A bookshelf held a series of fantasy novels, their spines cracked from multiple reads, and a collection of sporting trophies. She wondered what the labels read but finding that out would have to wait until Danny finished venting.

He stood near the bed with his hands linked on top of his head and stared at her with the same look of disbelief he'd flashed in the lounge. 'You went back last night, didn't you? Alone, after I'd gone.'

'I did.'

'Jesus, Beth.' He unlinked his hands and drew them over his face, before letting his arms flop to his sides. 'What time did you finish?'

'Late.'

'How late?'

'Just late.'

Danny's chest rose and fell on a deep sigh. 'I can't decide

whether to be furious with you or kiss you stupid.'

'The latter would definitely work better for me.'

He released a puff of laughter. 'I bet.'

'Don't be angry, Danny,' said Beth teasingly, tilting her head and curling her arms behind her back. The fabric of her dress tightened across the bodice. 'It's Christmas.'

His eyes darkened as he took in her pose, then in a rapid, sexy move that made her insides flip-flop and adrenaline rush her body, he crossed the room to land his hands on the wall either side of her head. Heat flamed from his body, igniting hers in return.

'At Christmas you're supposed to be nice,' he said, breath caressing her cheek and neck, not quite nuzzling, but close. 'You've been very naughty.'

'Only a little bit.'

His gaze flicked to her lips, then lower. Beth's skin puckered as though he'd stroked her. Danny edged even closer, his focus returning to her mouth. Slowly, he scanned upward. 'Thank you.'

Those looks, his closeness, his *hunger*, were setting her on fire. Beth tried to keep her voice normal but her words came out husky. 'You're very welcome.'

One corner of his mouth lifted. He was so close his shirt sleeves were brushing the bare skin of her arms, lifting the tiny hairs as though they'd been electrified. The scent of him made her dizzy with longing. He angled his head the other way, like a wolf contemplating where to bite first. Beth's nipples were tightening so hard they felt in danger of poking through her dress.

'I thought you wanted to kiss me stupid?'

'I do.'

'Well?'

'Now who's being bossy?' he murmured before closing his mouth over hers.

It was a slow kiss, lingering and tender, although not for long. As Beth's arms curled around his neck and Danny's body folded against hers, the kiss rapidly morphed into something deeper and hotter. The kitchen chatter and laughter faded, overtaken by the sounds of their breaths and soft gasps.

Danny's hand slid to Beth's thigh. He cupped the underside and lifted it, fitting himself close between her legs, fingers slowly sliding upward. 'This dress . . .'

Beth couldn't answer, her brain was too focused on the hardness of his arousal and the determined but gentle touch creeping up her thigh. She made a noise of want that had Danny moving his lips down her throat, then trailing nibbles to her ear before kissing his way back along her jaw to her mouth.

A knock sounded at the door. 'Danny?'

He groaned softly. 'Yeah, Mum?'

Beth closed her eyes. What was she thinking? It was Christmas Day and she was a guest, yet here she was getting hot and heavy with Danny in his bedroom. Not exactly the good impression of her plans.

'Sorry to interrupt. Your sister's out the back with Hobbles and fit to burst. You'd better come before she does.'

'Yeah, all right.'

Danny pressed his forehead against Beth's. 'Sorry.'

'We shouldn't be in here anyway.'

'Your fault. You disobeyed orders.' He stroked the sensitive skin of the inside of her thigh, shooting tingles north. 'I had to drag you off for a talk.'

'You call this talking?'

He grinned. 'Yeah. Secret Santa language.'

Beth broke into a giggle.

'God, you're gorgeous when you laugh.' He smoothed her hair back from her face and stared at her for several heartbeats, his voice lowering to a wonder-filled whisper. 'My gorgeous, special saddler girl. What a Christmas present.' For a long moment Danny seemed as lost in feeling as Beth, then he blinked and collected himself. 'I guess we'd better go see Ebs.' Kissing her one last time, he stepped back to straighten his clothes, grumbling at Beth's amusement over his discomfort. 'You wait, missy. It'll be your turn later.'

Given how aroused she was feeling herself, Beth certainly hoped so.

When he was satisfied the worst was covered up, Danny took her hand and led her back down the hall. The grandmothers cast them knowing smiles as they passed through the kitchen. Beth checked the others' expressions for disapproval and to her relief found none. Perhaps she shouldn't be surprised. They were both adults, after all, and while she might be the first girlfriend Danny had ever brought home for Christmas, Beth wasn't so naive to think she was the first he'd ever had in his room.

Ebony was waiting with Hobbles in the back yard. Dragging

the pony's head away from the grass it was greedily snatching, she bounced towards them. The pony's thick forelock had been plaited and tied in a knot to show off the newly fitted browband of her bridle.

'Doesn't it look great?'

'It does,' said Beth, inspecting the fit, pleased when it seemed to be fine. The browband itself looked a little over the top for her liking but there was no doubt Ebony loved it. 'Maybe we should do him a noseband to match.'

'No,' said Danny.

Ebony stared pleadingly at her brother. 'But—'

He cut his hand through the air. 'Nup, no, nyet. Beth's done enough of the bloody things. She needs a break.'

'The saddlery will be quiet after Christmas,' said Beth. 'I'm sure I'll have time.'

'Any spare time you have you'll be spending with me.'

Beth raised an eyebrow. Truth was she found Danny's assertive act sexy, mostly because she knew how kind-natured he was beneath, but that didn't mean she'd let him boss her around without a return fight. 'Will I just?'

'Yes.' Danny narrowed a look at his sister. 'No noseband, Squirt. Got it?'

Ebony returned fire with one of her teenage sneers. 'All right.' Then she flapped her arms and grinned. Hobbles, clearly used to drama, didn't flinch. 'I knew it, I knew it!'

'Knew what?' asked Beth.

'That you two were perfect for each other! You just needed to meet!'

'Are you telling me this was only about matchmaking?'

Beth didn't know whether to laugh or sob. Hours and hours of slaving over Ebony's browband, panicking she'd never get the job done, and it was all for a teenager's romantic fantasy?

'No, no,' said Ebony, catching her expression. 'Not just matchmaking. I really wanted the browband too. Truly-ruly.'

'You better have,' said Danny. 'Beth went through a lot to make that for you.'

'I know.' Ebony took Beth's hands. 'Thank you.'

Beth felt the warmth of her sincerity. 'I suppose I should thank you too.' She glanced at Danny and back again. 'I wouldn't have met Danny otherwise.'

Ebony giggled and released Beth's hands to cock both forefingers at her brother. 'You owe me.'

'I owe you nothing, ratbag. Now put Hobbles away and go help Mum.' When Ebony was out of earshot Danny curled arms around Beth's waist and drew her close, finally allowing his amusement to show. 'We probably do owe her.'

'We do.' Beth draped her own arms over his shoulders, pairing them like dancers. Under the day's gloriously blue sky, with Danny pressed against her, she felt like dancing. She smiled teasingly. 'I should really make her the noseband in thanks.'

'You should really not. Until your grandparents come back you're all mine.' Danny glanced over her shoulder and grimaced. 'We've an audience.'

'Let me guess, your grandmothers.'

'Yep, and assorted aunts and uncles.' A wrinkle appeared between his brows and his tone darkened. 'And Numbnuts.'

Beth smiled at the nickname. 'Not feeling brotherly love today? No peace on earth, goodwill to men?'

'Not when he's looking at your legs like that.'

'He's only doing it to wind you up.'

'I know, but he can still bugger off.'

'Possessive.'

'When it comes to you, you bet I am.' He pressed his forehead against hers. 'Can't help it. I'm crazy about you.'

Beth dragged her teeth over her bottom lip. 'Are you always this sure of things?'

'With the things that matter, yes. And you definitely matter.' He grinned and kissed her, then glanced at his watch. 'Lunch is at one. We've just under an hour. Feel like a ride?'

Ten

Danny couldn't keep his hands off Beth. The journey around the farm on the quad bike had brought colour to her lightly freckled cheeks and a windswept sexiness to her long hair. She looked bright, outdoorsy and prettier than ever, and to top it off his family adored her. Beth had charmed them with her cheerfulness, interest, and willingness to pitch in. Even his grandmothers were impressed.

With every look, every touch, every kiss, every *breath*, Danny's possessiveness deepened. He'd never felt like this with anyone else, but he'd never had a clock ticking on a relationship before and it was making him fearful.

Beth flashed him a weary but tolerant smile as Ebs dragged her off to talk to her equally horse-mad cousin Sienna. They were in what the Burroughs family called the Queensland Room — an aluminium extension enclosed on three sides with sliding mesh doors that kept the bugs out and the breeze flowing. Lunch had been over half an hour ago, the trestle tables cleared and the food put away. The adults were flopped on a hodgepodge of chairs, stools and benches, while the kids sprawled on beanbags or cushions on the floor. Moans about full bellies and much-needed naps competed with Christmas carols crooning from the speakers someone had brought outside. Danny could see Beth was beginning to wilt but his sister was determined to talk horse. Five more minutes and he'd rescue her.

Nick wandered to Danny's side, beer in his hand. He eyed Beth and shook his head. 'How the hell you got a girl like that will be forever one of life's mysteries.'

'No mystery. Smarter, better looking, usual shit.'

'Yeah, right.'

They watched Beth chat animatedly with Ebs and Sienna, Danny feeling like he could burst with pride as well as humility. Nick was right. How the hell a gorgeous, clever girl like Beth could be with a simple country bloke like himself was a mystery. Whatever the reason, he was grateful. Grateful, humble, happy, and crazy in love. Forgetting he was standing next to his brother, Danny gave in to an indulgent sigh.

Nick took a suck of beer. 'So when's the wedding?'

'Very funny.'

'Not that funny. Pretty obvious you're nuts about each other.'

The comment made Danny wish he had his own beer to suck on. Yeah, they were nuts about each other, but it wasn't going to be that easy.

'Got to convince her to come back first.' He caught Nick's look. 'She's heading back to Sydney as soon as her grandparents come home.'

'That's fucked.' Danny knew Nick meant it too. The Burroughs boys might be engaged in an endless game of one-upmanship, but that didn't mean they didn't love and look out for one another.

'Yeah.' But not unfuckable. At least Danny hoped it wasn't.

The signs were positive. Beth loved the farm, loved the whole area. He could feel it in the joyful way she'd wrapped her arms around him as they toured the farm on the quad bike, her enthusiasm to learn more, the pointing and asking questions about the farm, the district. The admiring glow in her eyes.

Most of all he believed that she loved *him*. Beth mightn't have admitted it yet but he was damn certain he'd captured her heart, and the hope of it was exhilarating. Danny's challenge now was to make sure he kept that feeling alive. Without it he'd never get her to come back. Then they'd be well and truly fucked.

'We'll get there,' said Danny. He'd make sure of it. She *belonged*. He nodded towards Beth. 'I'd better go and rescue her.'

'But we were talking saddles,' whined Ebony when Danny extracted Beth from her and Sienna's fanatical clutches.

'You can talk more later. Beth needs a break.'

Ebony stuck out her lip. 'You just want her for yourself.'

'Yep, I do.' And in ways he had no intention of sharing with his little sister, or anyone else. As he helped Beth up, Danny pressed his mouth close to her ear so only she could hear. 'I know a spot.'

'I bet you do.'

'Not like that.' Though God knows he wanted exactly what that purry voice inferred. 'A place where you can rest up in quiet for a bit.'

She leaned his head against his shoulder. 'Thanks. I have to admit I'm flagging.'

He kissed her hair. 'I know. That's why I'm here.'

Danny led her outside and across the back lawn. His mum wasn't that much of a gardener but the lawn was lush and well-tended, and Judy appreciated a shady bower where she could escape from her boisterous family to read or relax for a while.

Beth sighed when she saw the triple-seater swing. Its yellow canvas awning and cushions might be faded and the steel frame sporting touches of rust, but it was comfortable and cool thanks to a pair of overhanging maple trees, both in magnificent full leaf.

'Beautiful,' she said.

'Not so much in the autumn when the leaves drop. You wouldn't believe the mess. They're pretty in colour though.' He kissed her temple. 'Not as pretty as you.'

'Flatterer.'

'Crazy about you. Come on, you can lie down and use my legs as a pillow and I'll swing you to sleep.'

'With lullabies?'

'If I have to.'

Danny sat first and helped Beth find a comfortable position. Her eyes closed almost immediately, allowing him to study her face, angelic in the shade and quiet. He stroked her forehead and hair, his chest feeling thick.

'I don't even know what kind of music you like,' she said softly.

'You're meant to be sleeping.'

She smiled and Danny had to stop himself from breaking his back trying to kiss her. 'I will. Until then we can talk for a while.'

'I like all sorts, rock mostly. Normal stuff.'

'No thrash metal?'

'Nah, not me.'

'Rap?'

'Nope.'

'Good. They're not my thing either.' She covered a yawn. 'Sorry.'

'Don't be. You had a late night.'

'I did.'

'Beth?'

'Mmm?'

The words 'I love you' hung on his tongue. Maybe later, after she'd rested. When he'd taken her home and they had the privacy to take the words and make them physical.

He leaned close instead. 'Go to sleep.'

'Hello, sleepy gorgeous girl,' said Danny as Beth blinked awake.

Their little bower had been so cool and quiet that Danny had dozed himself. He'd woken to find Beth still deeply asleep and spent the past ten minutes indulgently watching her. That had been broken by the sounds of children being let loose into the yard and the excitement of the Burroughs clan annual Christmas Day cricket bash.

Beth smiled, and then rolled her head aside, her hand flying to her mouth.

'Don't worry,' said Danny, amused, 'you didn't dribble. Snored a bit but only softly.'

Her nose screwed up at the news. 'Sorry.'

'Don't be. It was cute.'

'Snoring isn't cute.'

'It is when you do it. You do this kind of puppy snuffle. It's sweet.'

'Thanks.' She frowned. 'I think.'

Whoops sounded from the other side of the yard. The cricket game must have started. Danny supposed he should join in but he didn't want to break the moment, not with Beth on his lap, her silky hair cascading out, stopping his heart. Her legs were rested on the handrail and the angle caused her dress to slip up her thighs. Not provocatively, but enough to give him a taste of her smooth pale-gold skin. If they weren't in his parents' backyard, Danny would have stroked it. He would have done a lot more too.

Noticing the noise, Beth tried to sit up.

'Don't. Please.' He touched her cheek. 'A bit longer.'

She eased back down. 'Aren't your legs going to sleep?'

They'd gone dead ages ago but Danny wasn't about to admit it. 'They're fine.' He caressed her hair, so soft and long. He could play with it all day. He could play with *her* all day. 'Tell me about growing up in England.'

Beth shrugged and turned her gaze to the tree canopy. 'It was good. School, sport, friends. Usual stuff.'

Danny wondered what she was hiding. He hadn't forgotten her comment about escaping to a nearby riding school and sitting with the kind saddler when things were bad at home, or her easy dismissal when he'd tried to probe.

'And your parents?'

She fingered a button on her dress. 'Dad was away from home a lot. I think Mum found that hard. They used to argue about it.' She was silent for a moment. When she spoke there was a rough edge to her voice. 'My family is nothing like yours.'

'Mine's pretty full on.'

'I think they're wonderful.'

There was wistfulness there, longing, admiration, honesty. Danny continued to stroke her hair, his heart melting with sympathy that things clearly hadn't been great for her growing up. 'I'm sure yours was special too, in its way.'

Beth shook her head. 'I think my parents came to hate one another.'

'I'm sorry.'

Her eyes found his. 'Mum only stayed because of me. She wanted to come back to Australia but I was torn, and scared. I loved Mum but I loved Dad too, and England was what I knew, where my friends were. Then when I finished school and started my apprenticeship, and Mum finally left Dad, still she stayed on, even though her heart was in another country. We're not close like your family but I'm her only child.'

An only child. That explained a lot.

'Is that why you followed her back to Australia?'

Beth nodded. 'I felt like I owed her. I still do.'

'You feel guilty for all the years she stayed with your dad, when she was unhappy?'

Beth's lips thinned as she pressed them hard together and for a horrible moment Danny was certain she was going to cry, but then she inhaled a shuddery breath and smiled. Despite her vulnerability, his Beth was tough, which was another reason he loved her. And also why he was going to fix this. Somehow.

'Yes, but enough of me.' She poked his belly. 'I want to know more about you.'

'You already know it all. Big funny family, Numbnuts for a brother, meddling sister, cool mum and dad.' He grinned and wiggled his eyebrow. 'Snogs like a champion.'

She laughed. 'Conceited.'

He kissed his fingers and pressed them to her lips. 'Crazy about you.'

Beth's laughter broke off and her expression turned serious, her gaze intense. 'I'm crazy about you too.' Lines appeared between her brows. Her hand moved to his shirt and she fingered the fabric, staring at it. 'Danny, this past week . . .' She didn't go on.

'What?'

'Nothing. I'm going to miss you, that's all.'

'We'll see each other again. I'll take holidays, come up and visit.' He cupped her cheek. 'We'll make it, I promise. You and me, Santa and the saddler. We're the real deal,

Beth. The once-in-a-lifetime deal that people write songs about.'

She closed her eyes and Danny's guts churned with the fear that he'd pushed too far.

'Danny?'

'Yeah, gorgeous?'

'Take me home?'

Eleven

Beth should have realised that leaving the Burroughs wouldn't be easy. As soon as she and Danny appeared around the side of the house, the younger kids were on them, demanding they join their team.

'Beth needs to go home,' said Danny. 'She had a late night and a big week.'

Beth had taken in the disappointed faces and squeezed Danny's hand. It was Christmas, and not a time to be selfish. Besides, she and Danny would have all night. 'A couple of overs won't hurt.'

A couple of overs turned into five, then ten. Danny bowled gently to the young kids but when Nick came in to bat it was war. The brothers sledged each other mercilessly, Danny crowing and strutting when a bone-crunchingly fast ball sent Nick's stumps flying. Beth took an impressive catch in the outer that had Danny rushing over to kiss her silly, causing much cheering from the peanut-gallery of grandmothers and non-playing aunts and uncles.

When it was their team's turn to bat, Danny let his younger cousin Jordan choose the order. Jordan sent Danny in at number one, and himself at number two. The pair seemed hell-bent on winning the match themselves, gleefully smacking balls out of the yard and into the paddock beyond but it didn't last. Jordan was caught out for twenty-two and Danny, much to his annoyance, was bowled by a jeering Nick for eighteen, leaving them thirty-one runs left to win. Not much, but Danny's side consisted of three players under eight, Sienna, another teenage cousin who'd never displayed much athleticism, and an uncle and aunt who weren't much better, thanks to a few too many drinks over lunch. And Beth.

They still needed sixteen runs when she took the crease. Nick stalked the pitch, spinning the ball arrogantly in his hands while eyeing Beth with a curled lip.

'Don't even think it, Numbnuts,' warned Danny.

'Think what?'

'You know.'

Hiding a smile, Beth marked her crease and tried to look hopeless.

Although he took an intimidatingly long run up, the ball Nick sent down was slow and easy. Beth smacked it into the paddock, causing Danny to laugh and clap in delight and Nick to narrow his eyes. The second ball was slightly faster but the result was the same.

Nick raised an eyebrow at Danny, who lifted his hands and shrugged. 'Don't ask me.'

'You can play,' Nick accused Beth.

'I'm half English. Of course I can play.'

Cricket had been one of the few things Beth and her dad had done together when she was young. Every time he'd taken her to the local oval to practice bowling, batting and catching she'd felt special and loved. Now she was older, Beth suspected it had more to do with her dad escaping the house than father-daughter togetherness. The lessons petered out in her adolescence as her parents' marriage cracked further and then ceased all together, but her skills remained.

Nick shot another look at Danny and shook his head. 'Total mystery.'

'Yeah,' said Danny, grinning at Beth with pride. 'But a bloody brilliant one.'

Unfortunately, Beth was run-out for eleven when her young batting partner tripped over his feet and went sprawling, but Sienna proved surprisingly adept and scored the remaining runs with ease. Danny was elated, while Nick grumbled about ring-ins and cheating, but it was all good-natured fun. The younger players were praised by the gallery, the older ones teased with humour and love. Beth found herself lingering at the edge of the group and watching it with a combination of jealousy and longing.

Realising she hadn't followed, Danny regarded her with concern. 'You okay?'

She nodded. As a teenager, Beth had fantasised about having a family like this: large, tight-knit and adoring. Her parents loved her — she'd never doubted that — but they hadn't loved each other. Her English relatives lived too far away to get to know well and feeling she'd never been welcomed to the family, her mum hadn't encouraged visits either.

Danny walked towards her, his expression questioning.

'I was just thinking how lucky you are,' said Beth.

'I am,' he said, taking her hand and kissing her temple. 'I found you.'

She smiled and nudged his shoulder. 'I meant with your family.'

'I know. They're pretty special, although my brother has his moments. Do you want a drink or do you want to head off?'

'We can stop longer, if you want.'

'We could.'

Beth glanced at him. Danny's coffee-coloured eyes were alight. They both understood where this was leading, and both were hungry for it.

'Or?' she said.

'Or we could go.'

She smiled teasingly. 'And do what?'

Danny pressed his mouth close to her ear, his breath shooting thrills down her spine. 'Everything, Beth. Everything.'

Thanks to Danny stroking her waist and nuzzling her neck, unlocking her grandparents' front door proved as difficult as when they'd left that morning. Danny had kept his hand on her leg for most of the journey into Levenham, teasing her with his fingers and thumb, and steaming glances across the ute that promised plenty of pleasure ahead.

Finally she managed to fumble the key in the lock and push the door open. As soon as it closed behind them, Danny dumped their bags and pressed her against the wall, kissing her with a breathless intensity that made her toes curl and soft moans to tremble deep in her throat.

'God, Beth,' he said, groaning himself as his thumb brushed the underside of her breast. He dragged his mouth down her throat, moving his hand higher at the same time. The brush of his thumb over her nipple was electric.

Her hands went to Danny's chest, then ribs, then lower to burrow under his shirt. Tension flexed his muscles. His skin was hot. She wanted to feel, kiss and lick every centimetre of it. She wanted it next to hers.

Danny kissed and nibbled his way back up her throat and lifted his head, smiling. 'I don't suppose you have a bedroom handy.'

'I do.'

'Want to show me the way?'

'Not liking the wall?'

'Oh, I like the wall. I like anywhere you are.' He caressed her breast again and nuzzled the hollow of her neck, breathing her in. 'I've been thinking about this all day.'

So had Beth.

'Danny . . .' At her tone he looked up, frowning slightly. Beth bit her lip, feeling suddenly shy. 'Did you bring condoms?'

'Yep. A whole packet.' He grinned. 'Although the way I'm feeling, that mightn't be enough.'

'Promises, promises.'

'You bet. Not to be pushy, but this bedroom of yours . . .?'

'Is right this way.'

Beth led him by the hand. Her bed was unmade and her pyjamas were still on the floor thanks to her morning rush. Another time the untidiness would have annoyed her, but right now Beth's mind was on Danny and what they were about to do.

He placed his bag on a chair and unzipped it. Winking, Danny pulled out an unopened box of condoms and tossed it on the bedside table. 'Now,' he said, advancing towards her, brown eyes deepening to intense dark chocolate, 'where were we?'

Beth draped her arms around his neck and pressed against him. He was hard, very hard, and the feel of it shot her with anticipation. Breathless again and stupidly turned on, she moved her hips closer. 'Somewhere about here I think.'

'About time we got further along.'

'About time indeed.'

They shared a soft chuckle that was swiftly wiped away by Danny kissing her. His hands shifted from her shoulders, fingers tracing delicate teasing lines across her throat and chest until they settled at the top of her dress, then he lazily began to work the buttons. He made a game of it: each unbuttoning was followed by a series of playful explorations of newly exposed skin that set Beth even further on fire. Ever so slowly the bodice began to gape open. He slid the fabric over her shoulders and down, until it shimmied over her hips and fell to the floor, and Beth stood in her knickers and bra in front of him.

Danny paused to stare, lust hooding his eyes. 'Oh, man, look at you.' He stroked the hollow between her breasts. 'Perfect.'

'I want to see you too.'

Danny didn't need further encouragement. Still staring, he levered off his shoes, stripped off his shirt, unbuckled his belt and shorts and stepped out of them, then kicked the lot aside.

Beth pressed her palms against his chest, feeling the strength of his pectorals and the tickle of their light covering of hair. Smiling, she lowered her gaze to his trunks and sucked in a breath at the magnificent outline of his cock.

He touched her face and scraped back her hair, and smiled. 'Ready?'

'More than ready.'

His gaze became serious. 'I love you.'

'You don't have to—'

'I do, because it's true.'

Beth's throat thickened. She should be happy, thrilled, instead his declaration made her feel upset and overwhelmed. She blinked, wanting so much — a life with him, the chance of a future like she glimpsed today. Not knowing how to get it.

'Hey.'

'Can we just . . .'

Danny's smile was gorgeous, and filled with understanding and love. 'You bet we can.'

Twelve

As she roused from sleep, Beth became aware of something different. Her head was resting on a warm but firm and slightly hairy surface. Heartbeats pulsed under her palm. A strong arm circled her shoulder.

Danny.

She closed her eyes again and smiled to herself. Danny, Danny, Danny. What an afternoon. What a night.

The memory had her snuggling closer and hooking her leg over his. If it was possible, Beth would have burrowed inside his skin, he made her feel so amazing.

He dropped a kiss on her head. 'So you're awake at last.'

'Mmm.'

He laughed softly and gently repositioned Beth onto his chest so they could look at one another. Danny's hair was mussed from sleep and sex, his smile indulgent and satisfied, his velvet brown eyes full of love. Beth suspected she mirrored him. God knows, she felt wanton enough.

She folded her hands and rested her chin on them,

watching Danny's face while he traced letters on her back with his fingertips. She recognised an I, then an L, followed by an O, V and E, then a Y, O, U, and wished he could tattoo them there.

'How are you feeling?' he asked.

'Pretty wonderful. You?'

'The same.' He sighed dopily. 'Best Christmas ever.'

It had been for Beth too. 'And now it's Boxing Day.'

'Yeah. Any ideas on how to spend it?'

'Bed?'

He chuckled and reached under her arms to drag her higher up his chest, and kissed her. 'Girl after my own heart.'

'It wasn't your heart I was thinking about,' said Beth, kissing him back.

Kisses drifted into more lovemaking, easy and slow in the subtle morning shadows. Vaguely Beth wondered what the time was, then didn't care. It was precious time with Danny, and that's all that mattered.

They moved from the bed to the shower, then, deciding the day could wait a little longer, returned to bed. By the time Beth crawled out again, wobble-legged and laughing as Danny attempted to coax her back, she was starving. Other than a late night snack of chocolate biscuits, which had resulted in lots of smears, licking and giggles, they'd eaten nothing since Christmas lunch.

'I need food.'

Danny rested his hands behind his head, the sheet rucked around his hips, his smile smug as he unashamedly ogled her naked body. 'I could make a comment.'

'I'm sure you could.' She flicked his chest with a wet towel that had been left on the floor. They'd been terrible slobs, but housekeeping had been far from their minds. 'I meant proper food. Like . . .' She looked ceiling-ward, contemplating. There wasn't much food in the house, and what was there was far too healthy for her mood. What Beth craved was something naughty and indulgent, like a hamburger or fried chicken. 'I don't suppose there'll be any takeaways open?'

'Doubt it. Maybe the fish 'n chip shop at Port Andrews.'

He slid out of bed, Beth enjoying a good perve as he dug into his bag for fresh clothes. Danny was lovely to look at — long limbed, muscular and beautifully proportioned. In every department. In their unique ways, Beth's previous boyfriends had all been attractive, but nothing like Danny. His masculinity was effortless, and he was confident in his looks and body without being arrogant. Most of all he seemed built just for her. From the way his arms fitted around her shoulders, to the way their hands cupped together and their fingers entwined, and the way his lips seemed to know exactly where to travel over hers. The ease with which they made love.

They fitted in a way that was glorious and exhilarating, and when the time came, would be impossible to leave.

But like yesterday, now was not the moment to think of that. Now was the time to make the most of what they had.

'We could drive down there if you want,' he said, pulling a polo shirt over his head and wandering to the window to inspect the weather outside. 'Looks like a good day for the beach. Or I could duck home and grab stuff for a picnic. We could walk to the top of Mount Pitt, check out the view. Or climb Rocking Horse Hill.'

'Sounds energetic.'

Danny grabbed Beth from behind in a warm cuddle and worked kisses up the inside of her neck. 'Don't tell me you're worn out?'

'From you? Never.'

'Never?'

'Never.'

He sighed. 'God, I love you.'

Beth twisted in his arms to face him. 'I love you too.'

It was the first time she'd said it. His grin turned huge, his eyes tender and luminous. Reciprocated feeling pulsed from him like heat. With another dopey sigh Danny rubbed his nose against hers, then kissed her in that long, lazy, teasing way that made her legs turn to jelly.

When he pulled back, his expression had turned naughty. 'Say that again and I'll have to take you to bed.'

'What? With no lunch?'

'Oh,' said Danny, grinning wickedly, 'there'll be eating, don't you worry.'

'Love you, love you, love you.'

'Right,' said Danny, hoisting her easily over his shoulder in a fireman's lift and patting her bum. 'Here we go!'

In the end they settled for scrambled eggs on toast followed by fruit eaten on the back porch steps. Not exactly the greasy indulgence Beth craved but filling and, more importantly, enjoyed with Danny.

'Lawn needs a mow,' he said, squinting at the garden and biting into his apple.

'I know.' Beth broke off a piece of her banana and ate it as she scanned the neglected yard. Pop-up sprinklers had taken care of the watering and saved the lawn from death, but water combined with sunshine meant lots of growth, and the lawn had grown so long near the back edges that seed heads were threatening to form. A patch of clover had the temerity to take hold near the shed too. Poor Grandma, she'd be horrified to see her garden so unkempt. 'I haven't had a moment spare to do it. A job for tomorrow, after work.'

Danny swallowed then swapped the apple for Beth's banana. 'I'll sort it now, if you like.'

'Danny . . .'

'Won't take long,' he said, taking a bite.

'You don't have to look after me all the time.'

He passed back the banana. 'Yeah, I do.'

Beth was quiet for a while, the last piece of banana left untouched as she stared broodingly at the trees lining the back fence. She promised herself she wouldn't fret, but the knowledge she would soon be leaving, that she would lose this, kept bubbling to the surface. To have been shown so much, only to be unable to see how she could keep hold of it was hard to take. 'And when I'm gone?'

'I'll look after you then too. Whatever it takes, Beth.' He took her hand and squeezed it. 'You're worrying too much. We'll be okay, I promise.'

She forced a smile and finished off her fruit, but Beth's anxiety stayed with her through the remainder of the afternoon as she weeded and tidied, and Danny made short work of the front and back lawns.

'Mum rang,' he said, walking back out of the house with two tumblers and his mobile tucked into his front pocket. He handed Beth her drink. 'She wants to know if we want to come home for a barbie tonight.'

'Sure.' She raised the glass in a 'cheers' motion and swallowed some much-needed cool water. The early afternoon sun had yet to shift past the house and the yard was baking. 'Unless you don't want to.'

'I don't mind. We need to eat proper food and we don't have to stay long.'

'What time?'

'Seven, I guess. Maybe a bit earlier. Plenty of time. We can head down to Port Andrews, see if the shop's open and grab ourselves an ice cream.'

'We could.' Beth eyed him over the rim of her glass. 'Or we could amuse ourselves in other ways.'

Danny sidled closer. 'Other ways, huh?'

Beth draped one arm around his neck and smiled. 'Mmm.'

'I'm sweaty.'

'I know.' She drew herself close and nuzzled his neck. Danny smelled deliciously of fresh grass, sunscreen, and the soap they'd washed with earlier. She pressed harder against him, enjoying the rapidly increasing swell of his arousal against her belly. 'It's very sexy.'

His voice dropped to a hoarse whisper. 'You're very sexy.'

Then his mouth reached hers and Beth was swept once more on the tide of their love and passion.

'Seriously, Danny,' said Beth the following morning, 'there's no need for you to stay. I'll be fine on my own.'

They'd already had this argument earlier, when Beth had risen and readied for work, and asked Danny his plans for the day. When he'd answered simply 'You', Beth had reminded him there was a world out there that he needed to play in. It was the day after Boxing Day, the saddlery was bound to be dull and Beth doubted she'd see a single customer, particularly with the weather so hot. With Danny booked for a shift at the pub that night, staying would mean he'd be effectively working fourteen hours straight. They might have spent a lot of time in bed over the last day and a half, but it hadn't involved much sleep.

Danny had refused to back down. He'd driven her to the shop, followed her inside, and began helping to set up like it was something he did every day.

'You'll get bored,' said Beth, trying again when he'd finished wheeling out the plastic horse, still with Santa in his bronco pose. She'd have to think up something funny for New Year. Not that Beth expected to be here to celebrate it.

'With you? I doubt it.'

'But don't you have things to do on the farm?'

'Nope. Dad and Nick have everything under control.'

'What about your mum, your friends? Surely you have mates to catch up with?'

'Beth,' he said, cupping her cheeks and kissing her, 'I'm staying, so quit arguing about it.'

'But—'

'No buts. I don't know how much time we have left, but whatever it is, I'm going to spend as much of it as I can with the girl I love, okay?'

Heartfelt words that made her insides feel gooey and her heart full, and made further protest impossible. She released a long-suffering sigh to tease him anyway. 'Okay. If you insist.'

'I do. Now, let's count out this float.'

To Beth's surprise she did have customers that morning. Only a couple, and those were both returns of unwanted or wrong-fitting Christmas presents, but more than she'd expected. She and Danny spent most of their time in the workshop with music softly playing, and Danny doing his best to distract her from the non-urgent repairs she'd set aside in favour of her browband orders.

'Hungry?' he asked as Beth finally tied off the last stitch on the leather halter she was repairing.

She glanced at the clock and grimaced at how long the repair had taken, but it was hard to concentrate with someone's hands up your top. Beth had been left too absent-minded by Danny's sexy games to think of her stomach, but now he'd mentioned it, she realised she was peckish, and it was lunchtime.

'I am a bit. What do you have in mind?'

Danny's eyebrows wiggled. 'Lots of things.'

She batted him with a rolled up scrap of leather. 'Food wise.'

'Sandwiches from home, I guess,' he said with a shrug. 'You saw the fridge last night. It's still chockers.'

Beth had seen. Not only the main fridge but also the spare in the Queensland room where cold drinks were normally kept. Even though Judy had served more of the leftover salad with the barbeque, both fridges remained stuffed with food. When Beth and Danny went to leave, Judy had foisted a giant container of mixed roast meat, another of salad, and yet another of desserts on them, and it still barely made a dent.

'Will you be right for a while, while I go get it?' Danny said now.

'I'm sure I can manage.' She tucked the halter into its bag along with an invoice and carried it to the bench, only to be grabbed around the waist by Danny.

He pressed his forehead against hers. 'You'll miss me though.'

'Maybe.'

'What's this "maybe" business?'

'You know I'll miss you. But it also might give me a chance to get some work done.'

'Work, smerk,' he said, kissing her.

'Pays the bills.'

'It surely does, but it's Christmas holidays. And you know what they say.'

'What?'

'All work and no play makes Beth . . .?' He raised his eyebrows, waiting, eyes sparkling with laughter.

She tilted her head, gaze narrowed in warning. 'Makes Beth what?'

'A gorgeous girl,' said Danny, lifting her off her feet and twirling her around. Then with one last, lingering, toe-curling kiss, he was gone.

Beth stared breathlessly after him, hugging herself and high on love. She wandered to the front of the shop to watch his ute leave, missing him already. Pressing her head against the cool glass, she recalled how she'd done the same thing not many days ago, when she'd been overwhelmed by longing for a home like this, for community and inclusion, for love. Aware that circumstances meant it couldn't be.

The shop phone began to jingle. Beth smiled. She bet it was Danny, calling from the ute to tell her something silly.

'Lizzy-love,' said Grandpop when Beth picked up, 'good news. Your grandma's been given the all-clear to travel. We're coming home.'

Thirteen

Danny cranked up the volume of the radio in the ute. It was tuned to Levenham's version of a modern FM rock station, which really meant hits from every year since radio began. The Beatles were singing 'She Loves You' and his combined harmony bounced loudly around the cabin. Danny was glad he hadn't hit town yet or someone was likely to catch him making a tool of himself.

Not that he cared. Beth loved him. Nothing was going to puncture that bubble.

He glanced at the passenger seat. A white T-shirt sat on top of the plastic container of sandwiches and leftover pavlova he'd collected from home. On his way out of town, Danny had cruised Levenham's main street and noticed the single tourist shop open. Struck by an idea, he'd pulled over and ducked inside. Five minutes later he was out, an oversized I ♥ LEVENHAM T-shirt in his hand, grinning at his cleverness and contemplating all the ways he could con Beth into showing her thanks. She was good as showing her thanks. Very, very good, gorgeous saddler girl that she was.

Another thought had hit him at home, sending Danny rummaging in his mum's craft supplies until he found what he wanted—a squeezy tube of sparkly red fabric paint. Now the line '& Danny Burroughs' featured under the word Levenham. Not very neatly, but that wasn't the point. His name was there, and whenever she wore the T-shirt, she'd remember.

'I'm baaa-aack,' he yelled from the saddlery door, after checking the shop was empty of customers. 'With a special present for my sexy, clever saddler girl.'

No reply. Maybe Beth was waiting to surprise him with a present too. Her, naked on the workbench, would do.

Danny bounced across the shop and scooted behind the counter. Beth was sitting at the office desk staring at the screen of her grandfather's computer.

'Hey, gorgeous,' he said, kissing her cheek and nuzzling her neck. At her lack of response, Danny looked up, then his stomach plummeted to the floor as he clocked the airline website. He swallowed but his voice still came out wrong. 'When?'

'Sunday morning. Grandpop and Grandma are driving back tomorrow. There's only one flight out of Levenham on Sundays. I was hoping for something in the afternoon but—' Her voice cracked. Lowering her head, she hunched in on herself and rubbed at her arm.

'Oh, baby, shh.' Danny dumped his bags and curled her against his chest. 'Shh. It'll be okay. We'll be okay.'

Even as he said the words his heart was racing. Two

nights. That's all they had left, two nights, and he had to work both of them. Which left today and whatever time they could scramble together on Saturday before her grandparents returned. It wasn't enough.

'I'm sorry,' said Beth, sniffing. 'I want to stay longer but I can't. I have my job, Mum, car payments, rent due . . .'

'I know, baby. It's okay. I understand.' He held her face and made himself smile as though he believed everything was fine and his heart wasn't spilling longing and worry into his chest cavity. Danny had learned enough from his mates who'd had girlfriends go off to uni to know how tough long-distance relationships were, and how few of them lasted. Theirs would though. Now he'd found Beth, he wasn't letting her go. She was part of his heart. 'I'll come and see you. As soon as cricket season's over. I'll drive up for a week, longer.'

She blinked, her gaze huge, liquid, and worried. 'And then what, Danny? Then what? You'll return home and what?'

'And work some more and make plans to see you again.'

Beth twisted out of his grip and stared at the computer screen, her expression hollow. Danny hated that look. It was the look of someone who couldn't see the future and it made his guts clench and desperation creep a layer of cold sweat over his skin.

'Beth?'

She continued to stare.

Danny took a deep breath and used his finger to gently turn her face back to his. 'You could always stay.'

Her lips parted and for an exhilarating second he believed she might say yes, but then her eyes dulled and she shook her head. 'I can't leave Mum.'

'I know you feel guilty, but wouldn't she want you to be happy?'

'It's not that simple.'

'It can be, if you let it.'

She smiled and cupped her hand to his cheek. 'You are such a darling man, and you're right. We will be fine. We'll make it fine, like you said.'

Which was exactly what Danny wanted her to believe. So why did he feel like he'd just been fobbed off?

'In the meantime,' she said, voice high with false brightness, 'we'll just have to make the most of what we have. So, Santa, did I hear you mention a present?'

Danny hesitated and decided to take her on face value. He didn't want to spend what little time they had arguing anyway.

'You did. A bit late for Christmas, sorry. Seems Santa got distracted by a gorgeous girl.' He held the T-shirt high so she could read the transfer and his writing. 'What do you think?'

Beth frowned, as though not understanding, and lifted the hem for a closer look at his clumsy script. Then she began to laugh.

'You like it?'

'I love it.' She wrapped her arms around him, trapping the T-shirt between them. 'Like I love you. It's a great present.'

Danny pressed his cheek against hers, eyes closed as he held her close. 'I'd give you the world if I could.'

'I know you would. But this is enough for now.'

The afternoon went too fast. Danny spent most of it in the workshop, kissing and fondling Beth and feeling as randy as a spring buck rabbit. Several times they came to the brink of sex only for one of them to realise they'd gone too far and retreat. Then they'd laugh and feign control for a while until the teasing games started all over again.

To Danny's relief, the few customers that called in didn't stay long. As much as he wanted to help Beth he stayed hidden, unwilling to risk being accosted by someone he knew and having to make conversation when his brain was well and truly lodged in his trunks along with his hard-on. As soon as Beth dealt with them and reappeared at the workshop door, he opened his arms for her. The thrill of her grin, the way she skipped towards him, was a memory he'd hold onto for a long, long time.

He wanted time to stand still. He wanted five o'clock to come so he could have Beth without risk of interruption. Most of all he wanted her to stay forever.

Danny wanted, wanted, wanted.

But the only thing he could have was her body and heart, and thanks to his shift at the pub, enjoyment of the former was annoyingly curtailed. Mind-blowingly good, but still too damn short.

'Why don't you come to the pub tonight?' he asked.

They were in the shower. Danny didn't have time for more lovemaking but he couldn't stop sliding soap over Beth's beautiful chest. Her skin felt silky, her breasts pillowy, and the way the foam sat on her erect nipples was mesmerising. Another memory for his bank.

'And do what?'

Good question. She'd probably be chatted up all night by idiots, leaving Danny so cranky and possessive he'd end up cracking someone's head.

Beth pressed him against the tiles, hand cupping his balls and slowly stroking upward. 'Not this, I'm guessing.'

'No.'

She smiled, well aware of the effect she was having. 'Or this.'

Danny's eyes began to cross as Beth used her knowledge of his body to torment him even further. He supposed it was only fair. He'd spent all day doing the same to her in the saddlery workshop but, man, she was hot. Hot, horny and his.

'And definitely not this,' she whispered and began trailing her mouth down his chest.

By the time they made it out of the shower, the conversation had been obliterated from Danny's brain, but not Beth's. 'Do you still want me to come to the pub?'

He did. If the choice was between being without her, or suffering some tool trying to crack on to her in the pub, he'd choose Beth every time. He could always boot any potential Romeo's butt out, and jealousy was for insecure idiots. Which wasn't him. Much. Anyway, Danny could always make Beth wear her I ♥ LEVENHAM & Danny Burroughs T-shirt, or plonk a sign on her head saying 'Touch me and die'. That'd do the job.

'Yeah, I do. You up for it?'

'With you, Santa-man,' she answered saucily, 'I'm up for anything.'

Which only made Danny think of sex. Again. He rubbed his face and tried to get a grip. As always, other parts of him had different ideas.

This was going to be a very long night.

At the Arms, after introducing her to his colleagues Barry and Karen, Danny settled Beth on a stool at the far end of the bar, and fetched her a glass of wine and a bag of mixed nuts to munch on. It was just gone six and the pub was still quiet but would pick up quickly once people began arriving for dinner. Danny wasn't sure how much use he'd be. After laughing off his suggestion to wear his T-shirt, Beth had dressed in tight red pants that fitted every curve, and matched them with a white shirt that was far too flimsy for Danny's liking. When she bent forward, the neck gaped, exposing the pretty lace edge of her bra, and if she stretched an arm, tightening the fabric, more lace showed through.

Lace, bra, boobs. Boobs that less than an hour before had soap bubbles lathered on their peaked nipples.

He was going to go crazy thinking about it, that's if he didn't get himself sacked first for growling like a rabid dog at every bloke who even breathed in her direction.

Respite came in the arrival of his brother. Danny was so relieved he could have kissed him. Numbnuts might like to stir, but he'd protect Beth like a lion.

'What are you doing here?' Danny asked, pouring Nick a beer.

'Meeting Harry and Summer for dinner.'

'Do you mind if Beth joins you?'

'Nah. No probs. She'll stop me looking like a Nigel-no-friends.' Nick winked at Beth across the bar. Immune to his charms, Beth rolled her eyes, making Danny grin. Nick looked from his brother to Beth and back again. 'Fucking mystery,' he said, handing over cash and shaking his head.

'Fucking brilliant,' replied Danny, feeling about a hundred feet tall.

When Harry Argyle arrived with his pretty beautician girlfriend Summer, Danny took a break from serving to introduce Beth and was thrilled when Summer and Beth began chatting immediately. Although not from as far away as Beth, Summer was a relative newcomer to Levenham, and given how things had turned out for her — meeting Harry and getting in with Josh Sinclair and his wife Em's crowd, who were all good people — she was bound to put a positive spin on the place.

'So how do you all know each other?' asked Beth.

'Cricket.' Danny nodded at Harry. 'This big lump's my team's vice-captain.'

'And footy,' said Harry. 'Arch rivals. I play for the mighty Gerrinton Giants and those two,' he indicated Danny and

Nick, 'play for Mount Pitt, better known as The Pitts.'

'Mighty, my arse,' sledged Nick.

'Who's mighty?' interrupted a voice, the owner of which immediately lit on Beth. 'Hello.'

Danny groaned inwardly as he recognised Harry's brother Eddie. Almost the same height as his giant sibling and built just as solidly, Eddie was a self-proclaimed pants man. Although not very good at it.

'Hello,' Beth said warily.

'Is that an English accent I hear?' When Beth nodded, Eddie thrust his hand out, grinning. 'I'm Eddie.' He tilted his head at Harry. 'This idiot's better-looking brother. And you are?'

'My girlfriend Beth,' said Danny.

'Girlfriend?' Eddie stared between Beth and Danny then raised his eyebrows at Nick.

'Yeah,' said Nick. 'Fucking mystery to me too, mate.'

'Piss off,' Danny growled.

Beth shook Eddie's hand and quickly released it. 'What is it with this town and brothers? You all think you're better than one another.'

Which brought on a chorus from the men of variations on 'That's 'cos we are,' and caused Summer and Beth to share a rolly-eyed look.

'Ignore him,' said Danny, jerking his thumb at Eddie. 'He's a sleaze.'

Eddie stiffened. 'Am not.'

Everyone stared at him.

'I just like pretty girls,' said Eddie, head turning as a

blonde strutted past towards the bistro, before winking cheekily at Beth, who laughed.

Danny was about to tell him to lay off when Barry tapped his shoulder and indicated the bar. The dinner crowd had arrived. He grimaced, then shot a warning glare at Eddie. 'You,' he cocked a finger, 'don't even think it.' His expression softened as he focused on Beth. 'Have fun, babe.'

She smiled back, eyes full of him. 'Don't work too hard.' Then she stood and leaned across the bar to whisper, 'I don't want you falling asleep on me later.'

'Never,' he whispered back, sneaking in a kiss.

'What did I say?' muttered Nick again, as Danny turned aside to take an order. 'Fucking mystery.'

'No mystery,' Danny overheard Beth say with deliberate sweetness. 'Snogs like a champion and is hung like a horse. Not much else a girl needs, really.'

For a pause there was astonished silence, then the corner of the bar exploded with laughter, leaving a grin on Danny's face that lasted an hour and implanting another gorgeous memory of Beth in his lovesick heart.

'Your friends are nice,' said Beth as Danny drove as fast as the speed limit allowed to her grandparents'.

'Of course they are. I'm a nice bloke.'

'You are.' She reached across to tug on his ear. 'Also conceited.'

'What happened to snogs like a champion and hung like a horse?'

'I may have exaggerated.'

Danny shot her a look.

Beth grinned. 'Okay, so I told the truth. You're still conceited.'

'Nah, I'm just crazy about you and trying to impress.'

'You don't have to try. I'm impressed.'

Danny stroked her cheek. 'Love you.'

'Love *you*.'

'Love you more.'

'Do not.

'Do.'

The silly argument lasted all the way into the house, where Danny silenced it by kissing Beth breathless. The house echoed with their giggles as they clumsily shed clothes and tripped their way to her bedroom.

'I don't want tonight to end,' whispered Beth afterwards as Danny cuddled her.

Danny didn't either. With her grandparents arriving home tomorrow this would be their last night. No more laughing sex, no more delighting in Beth's gasps, the sexy little mewls she made, the murmur of his name that made his chest feel like it'd explode it was so full of love for her.

He kissed her silky hair, yet another thing he'd miss. 'Me either.'

'I wish you didn't have to work tomorrow night.' Her fingers curled in his chest hair. 'Why do you work there anyway?'

'Money,' he said simply.

'Don't they pay you enough at Levenham Windmills?'

'Yeah, but I'm saving up.'

'For what?'

'Her' is what he wanted to answer. For a dream home for his dream girl. 'A place of my own. House on a few acres. Not too many, ten maybe. Enough space to muck around in, but not so much it's a pain to look after.' He shrugged, afraid to add the rest about places for kids to play and ride horses and motorbikes. 'I've had enough saved for a deposit for a while now, just haven't found the right place. One'll turn up though. In the meantime, I'll just keep working and saving.'

'That sounds wonderful.'

He looked down but Beth was curled against him and he could only see the top of her head. 'You must have a dream too. Something you're working towards.'

'Not really.'

'Come on, Beth, everyone has dreams.'

She continued to toy with his chest hairs. 'I guess I'd like my own saddlery one day.'

'I figured that'd be high on your list. What else?'

She moved restlessly, as if the conversation made her uncomfortable. Maybe it did, but if Danny didn't know her dreams, how could he give them to her?

'What else?' When she still didn't answer, he shifted down the bed until they were face to face. 'What else do you dream of, Beth? What's really in your heart?'

Her eyes were shiny when she answered, her voice husky as though the admission caused her pain. 'I dream of a family like yours. One that doesn't fight or yell or hate, or makes their children feel guilty or frightened or sad. Just a normal loving happy family, the way they're meant to be. That's not too much to ask, is it?'

'No,' said Danny, holding her close and feeling on the verge of pain himself. 'No, it's not.'

Fourteen

Beth was doing her best to stay upbeat for Danny, but inside her heart was breaking. She was exhausted, too. They'd hardly slept the previous night, too afraid to sleep in case they missed precious seconds with one another.

To make matters worse, her admission to Danny about wanting a family like his had left Beth feeling hollow and mean. It was a betrayal of her parents, who, although their own relationship was deeply flawed, had done their best to love their daughter. Except for a pony of her own, Beth had never wanted for anything. She'd lived in a nice house in a beautiful part of England, attended a good school, her clothes were all new, and when she was younger she'd had piano and ballet lessons. No one had hit her, and other than at each other, her parents had rarely even yelled. Hardly a deprived childhood. But it had sometimes been lonely, occasionally frightening and often heavily weighted with guilt. The hankering for that close-knit loving family circle that many of her friends took for granted had always tugged at her heart, but that didn't give her permission to disrespect her own.

Saturday morning was busier in the shop. Knowing Danny wouldn't budge whatever she said, Beth didn't bother trying to convince him to leave her to it. She didn't want him to go anyway.

As the morning drifted, Beth kept sneaking glances at the time, mentally counting down the hours until her flight left. When she wasn't serving or tidying for Grandpop, she was kissing Danny like it was their last. Soon it would be.

When closing time came at twelve, Beth counted the takings and stowed them in the safe, along with the following Monday's cash float. She checked the workshop door and windows, and, finally satisfied, walked on leaden feet to the front door. She paused and looked back, absorbing the shop's old-fashioned welcoming atmosphere into her skin, inhaling its unique and comforting scent, wishing she could bottle both.

Her eyes were stinging when she set the alarm. By the time she turned the key in the lock, tears were falling.

'Hey, shh,' said Danny, holding and soothing her as she snivelled onto his chest in the car park. 'It's okay.'

It wasn't okay, and she wasn't convinced it ever would be, but she had to stop being a coward and find faith. Danny deserved better than her doubt.

Beth sniffed back her tears and gave him a wobbly smile, then stared at the door. 'Remember that night?'

'How could I forget.'

'I'll never look at Santa the same way again.'

'I'll have to remember to wear my suit when I come and see you, relive the moment.'

That made her smile properly. 'You're so cute. Silly, but cute.'

'I know.'

'Conceited.'

'Crazy about you,' he said kissing her hard, then backed off with a grin as a car full of lads drove past, whooping. 'What time are your grandparents due?'

'Around two.'

'Plenty of time.'

'For what?' she said, although Beth suspected she already knew the answer.

He shucked her under the chin. 'Not what you think, my gorgeous sexy saddler girl.'

Instead of taking her home, Danny drove to Port Andrews, where he bought fish and chips and carried them to the spot where they'd first kissed. The day wasn't as perfect as then. The wind was up, whipping and tangling Beth's hair and rapidly cooling the chips, but the seagulls were as ravenous and calamitous, and the air was scented with salt and seaweed and Norfolk Island pine. Most of all, Danny was there, still sparking with attraction, still holding certain that they were meant to be, despite her protests.

'What a Christmas,' he said, snuggling his body against hers. They were stretched out on the grass, their lunch finished, the rubbish binned. They should have been driving back to Levenham in case her grandparents arrived early, but Beth didn't want to leave. He grinned, his brown eyes flashing amber highlights in the sun. 'Didn't I promise you Christmas magic?'

'You did, and you delivered.'

'Santa always delivers.' He sobered. 'Promise me something?'

'Of course.'

'Keep believing in us. Even when you think it'll never work out, remember now, remember all we've shared, and trust that we can still have it. I know you have doubts, I can see them in your eyes, and I know you're worried about your mum and don't want to leave her, but we love each other, Beth. We're meant to be. And if the universe doesn't sort a way for us to be together, then we will. It won't happen tomorrow, or even next week, but it will, I know it will. But I need you to believe too.' He touched the tear that had fallen from her eye. 'Promise me. Please.'

Beth's voice was a cracked whisper. 'I promise.'

Beth was at the front of her grandparents' house trying their mobile for the third time when they pulled into the yard.

'Sorry we're late, Lizzy-love,' said Grandpop. 'Took a bit longer than expected. Had to let your grandma out for a few stretches along the way.' He hugged Beth tightly. 'How's my girl?'

'All the better for seeing you. Why didn't you answer your phone?'

'Didn't hear it.' He winked. 'Probably because it was in the boot.'

Beth laughed. How typical. 'So how are you? Okay after your long drive?'

'Oof, a bit stiff, but not bad for an old fella.' He nodded towards the passenger side. 'We'd better help Lynn out.'

After hugging her grandma and helping her inside, and several trips to unload the car, Beth settled her grandparents in the kitchen and put the kettle on. She raided the fridge, and laid out a container of Judy's lemon slice.

Grandma inspected it closely, then regarded Beth with delight. 'Have you been baking?'

'No, they're courtesy of Judy Burroughs.'

Her grandparents exchanged a look.

'I hear you and the Burroughs lad have been quite friendly,' said Grandma, more than a little slyly.

Friendly wasn't quite the word, given the amount of sex they'd indulged in, but Beth could hardly describe how intense her relationship with Danny had really been. 'Who have you been talking to?'

'Everyone,' said Grandpop with a chuckle. 'You know your grandma and her local grapevine.'

'Are you calling me a gossip?'

Grandpop threw up his hands. 'Would I ever do that, my love?'

Beth smiled at their banter. They were so cute. Her mind immediately drifted to Danny, wondering what he was doing. She'd asked him for this time alone with her grandparents. He'd protested, and it had hurt her heart, but apart from the half-day they'd spent together after she'd flown in to look after the saddlery, Beth hadn't seen them.

Before then it had been months, when they'd journeyed to Sydney on Beth and Curtis's urging to surprise Mum for her fiftieth birthday. It seemed unfair not to give them her full attention.

It had only been a couple of hours and already she missed him. What the coming weeks would be like she didn't want to contemplate.

'He's a good lad, young Danny,' said Grandpop, when Beth made no comment and feigned acute interest in making tea. Her back was to the table but she could feel her grandparents' curiosity in the lift of the hairs on the back of her neck. God, she hoped they never realised what Beth and Danny had done in their house. That would be too humiliating.

'Nice family,' agreed Grandma. 'Solid. Been around for a long time.'

'Plenty worse out there,' said Grandpop.

Beth placed a trivet in the centre of the table and set the teapot on top. 'Have you two finished?'

Grandma looked at Grandpop. 'Have we?'

Grandpop pursed his lips. 'Probably not.'

Though they tried, Beth wouldn't be drawn any further on Danny. She didn't want to give them hope, and despite her promise to him, she couldn't help feeling frightened of her own longing. Like Danny, her grandparents would love to have Beth stay, but the barriers seemed insurmountable. Financially, she couldn't afford it. With her car loan and rent, plus ongoing bills, she needed her job. What savings she'd once had had been gobbled up on relocation expenses, leaving her with little buffer. If she'd had one, things might be different, but the situation was what it was.

As for the emotional issues, they made Beth's heart feel carved out. She loved her mum, had moved across the world to be with her, and hold her hand as Angela took one of the biggest chances of her life with a man she'd only known six months. Beth couldn't just abandon her, not after the sacrifices she'd made, the years of misery. It wouldn't be fair.

After a long catch-up on Lynn's injury and rehabilitation, her aunt's health, and other family news, along with a detailed report from Beth on the saddlery, followed by a light dinner of Burroughs Christmas leftovers, her grandparents retreated to the lounge and the telly. Beth joined them, but no matter how she tried to relax into their easy banter, she was gripped by restlessness.

At a quarter to eight, Beth cleared her throat. 'Grandpop, do you mind if I borrow the car for an hour or so?'

'Of course not. Take as long as you need. Lynn and I were planning an early night anyway.'

'You should have invited Danny around for tea,' said Grandma, when Beth bent to kiss her.

Beth flushed at how obvious her hunger for him was. 'He's working tonight.'

'Hard worker, that lad,' said Grandpop, his tone approving. 'Like yourself. Make a good match.'

Beth shook her head. 'You two . . .'

Grandma patted her hand. 'Just helping.'

'I know you are, and you're lovely.' But it only made Beth's heart heavier.

Instead of turning toward the Arms, Beth headed for the saddlery. An hour later, she was back in the car and driving towards Danny.

'Hey,' said Danny, looking up in delight and leaning across the bar to kiss Beth. 'I wasn't expecting you.'

'I hadn't planned on being here.' She glanced at the bar. A few patrons waited to be served, but most appeared to be propped on stools or leaning against the timber edge, enjoying their drinks and chatting. Busy but not unmanageable. 'Do you have a minute?'

His brow furrowed. 'Everything all right?'

'Yes, I just want to talk to you in private a minute.'

Danny assessed the crowd, fingers tapping as he did. 'I should be right. I'll just need to tell Barry.'

Seconds later he was steering Beth out the front door. They stood to the side of one of the windows so Danny could keep an eye on the bar while they talked.

He gave the pub one last check and focused on Beth. 'I'm glad you're here.'

'I couldn't stay away.'

'I know the feeling.' He smiled sheepishly. 'I drove past your place on the way to work, hoping to catch a glimpse of you.'

His eyes locked with Beth's sending her heart tumble-turning. She wanted to speak but the words had dried up with the love she saw there.

A shout from down the street broke the moment and she

smiled. 'I have something for you.' She reached into her pocket for the bracelet she'd made. 'Hold out your arm.'

'Which one?'

She pursed her lips and decided. 'Left.'

He held it out. Carefully she wrapped the plaited leather bracelet around his wrist and knotted it into place, then traced her fingers over the surface.

'I wove my hair into it.' She looked up. 'So you'll have me near you all the time.'

He touched it, tracing the weave as she had. His eyes were limpid from the street light and the window's glow. His Adam's apple bobbed as he swallowed deeply. 'Thank you. It's perfect.' He cleared his throat and gave a wobbly smile. 'Makes my T-shirt look pretty ordinary.'

'Your T-shirt is wonderful.' She reached on tip-toe to kiss him. 'You're wonderful.'

His arms folded around her. 'You are. You're the best, most perfect, gorgeous girl and I am so, so lucky to have you in my life.'

Beth was sniffing back tears when he set her down, and from the flush on his cheeks and the way he softly cleared his throat, she had the feeling Danny was too.

'I'd better let you get back to work.'

He glanced inside and made a face. 'Yeah.' Then he looked at her and sighed, but in a happy way. 'I love you.'

'I love you too. See you tomorrow?'

'Wouldn't miss it.' With a last kiss and a tender stroke of his hand down her face, he returned to the bar.

Beth stood on the footpath watching him through the

window, until her tears of longing had dried and the rising southerly wind blew goosebumps across her flesh. Then she crossed her arms over her bleeding heart and headed for the car.

Fifteen

The southerly change that Beth had felt the tip of the previous night had arrived in force, sending the temperature plummeting. Around Levenham's small airport terminal, people squinted distrustfully at the cloudy sky outside and grumbled as they dug jumpers and cardigans out of carry-on luggage in preparation for the walk to their plane.

Noticing her shiver, Danny wrapped warm arms around her and kissed her neck while Grandpop and Grandma exchanged an indulgent smile.

'I'm here,' he whispered, 'keeping you warm with my loving arms.'

Beth smiled. Danny was such a hopeless romantic. On the tarmac, a baggage handler was loading suitcases into her plane's hold as the pilot ran his check, while inside a male attendant behind the airline's desk ticked items off a list. They had minutes left. Seconds. Heartbeats. And with every one of them, Beth's throat thickened and her eyes prickled.

Danny had arrived early at the house, bearing a container

from Judy stuffed with food for Beth to eat on the way, instead of horrible airline snacks or overpriced terminal junk food. He also had a battered copy of *The Silver Brumby* from Ebony, an Australian classic which Beth had admitted on Christmas Day she'd never read. Both kindnesses had almost brought her undone.

'I think we're up,' murmured Danny as the attendant lifted a microphone.

The boarding announcement echoed tinnily through the terminal. People turned to one another, sharing hugs, kisses and handshakes. Beth swallowed and eased from Danny's embrace, straightening her shoulders. She glanced at him, taking strength from his nod of encouragement, and stepped forward to make her farewells.

'Next time,' whispered Grandma, patting Beth's back and leaving moisture on her cheek. Beth understood. Next time they'd have more time together. No broken hips, no other people to care for. Just them.

'Definitely next time, Grandma.' She kissed her and gave her stern look. 'You make sure you let Grandpop take care of you so you can let that hip heal properly. I don't want to hear of any setbacks, okay?'

Beth moved on to her grandfather. Not having to balance on a cane like Grandma, his embrace was even fiercer.

'Thank you,' he said in a choked voice. 'It was a wonderful thing you did for us.'

'It was my pleasure, Grandpop. All my pleasure.'

He held her at arm's length, his eyes watery. 'You come back soon, Lizzy.'

'I'll do my best.'

With a shuddery exhale and a nod, Grandpop let her go. Beth turned to Danny and caught his hands.

'I'll miss you,' she said.

'I'll miss you too, but I'll come up. As soon as I can.' He pressed his forehead against hers, smiling past his sadness. 'We'll make it, Beth.'

Danny glanced up and his expression clouded. Beth checked over her shoulder. The attendant was watching them, pen tapping his clipboard. Beth had a childish urge to poke her tongue out at him.

She stayed focused on the attendant, frowning and scraping her teeth over her lip. How easy it would be to shake her head, apologise, and ask for her luggage to be unloaded. She closed her eyes and then opened them, and with a deep breath faced Danny with a smile as broken as her insides.

'I'd better go.'

'Yeah.' Danny held her face. 'I love you.'

'I love you, too.'

His kiss was brief but electric with feeling, leaving Beth trembling with doubt at her decision, and cursing that circumstances left her little choice. Danny lifted her backpack on her shoulder. She settled it and stepped backwards to the gate, gaze sweeping over the people she loved as she fixed them in her mind. Grandma was openly crying. Grandpop had his arm around her, no tears but his bottom lip wobbling. Danny stood straight-shouldered, strong and handsome. His expression was stoic, with only the brightness of his eyes betraying his true feelings.

She lifted a hand and gave a watery smile, then kissed the tips of her fingers and blew the kiss towards them. Grandpop nodded, Grandma sobbed and flapped her damp hanky. Danny touched his heart and mouthed 'I love you.'

Beth paused, soaking up the moment, soaking in their love, then she turned her back and walked through the gate. A cold gust splattered the tears on her cheeks and tore at her hair as though invisible hands were trying to pull her back. Gritting her teeth against her superstitious thoughts, she trudged on. At the plane steps Beth gave a final wave, and though she couldn't see into the terminal she knew they were there, waving back. With a last breath of Levenham's country-fresh air, she stepped into the aircraft.

As the plane taxied, Beth watched the terminal from her window. She watched as they lifted into the sky, as they banked and straightened, as the terminal and then Levenham faded to a cluster of coloured roofs and indistinct roads. Though she couldn't see Danny or Grandpop or Grandma, she kept vigil until the plane banked east and everything was lost from view.

🎁🎁

It was late afternoon when Beth arrived at her flat. Her skin was greasy with sweat and travel grime, and she wanted nothing more than a long shower and a glass of something cold, followed by the comfort of her bed, where she intended to have a good cry before falling into unconsciousness.

Unlike Levenham and then Melbourne, Sydney was hot

and revoltingly sticky. The airport had been clogged with tired travellers, the train to Central and then Hornsby even more congested with fed-up commuters.

Angela and Curtis had been waiting out the front of the station. Her mum hugged her with such ferocity it filled Beth with guilt that she'd even thought about not returning. Curtis had smiled and kissed her cheek, then took her luggage.

'You should come home with us,' her mother had admonished in the car. 'There'll be no food in your flat.'

Curtis had caught Beth's eye in the rear-view mirror. 'We can drop by the supermarket. Grab some basics.'

Beth smiled at him in gratitude. She was weary and heartsick and had to work tomorrow, and as much as she was thrilled to see her mum and Curtis, coming home still felt like a mistake. The past month had been her happiest since arriving in Australia. It wasn't only Danny, it was Levenham itself, the relaxed community and beauty of the landscape. It was working in a job where she could be creative and innovative, where she could talk to customers instead of toiling like a slave out the back. It was a place where Beth could dream.

She'd returned to gazing out at the suburban sprawl. The northern suburbs were leafy and pretty, but they weren't Levenham. Yearning, she rested her head against the glass and closed her eyes as her mum continued to chatter about their New Year plans. Beth had none. Stop home, sleep, talk to Danny.

Miss him.

The flat was stuffy and stale. Angela and Curtis helped pack her groceries away and unlock and open windows. Then they stood awkwardly in the tiny kitchen as her mother fussed. Beth's phone beeped as another message from Danny came in, wanting to know if she was free to talk yet. They'd been in contact every leg of the journey and it still didn't feel enough. She touched the image on her screen: Danny beaming. She wished he'd beam himself here for her to hold.

'I think Beth wants a shower and bed,' said Curtis.

'That sounds blissful,' she said. 'It's been a long day and I have an early start tomorrow.'

'Oh,' said Angela. 'Of course. Now, is there anything else you need? We can do another supermarket run. Get you stocked up for the week. Won't take long.'

'I'll be fine, Mum. I can grab some more supplies after work tomorrow.'

'All right then. Now, you're definitely coming for New Year?'

Figuring she must have missed a conversation somewhere, Beth glanced shiftily at Curtis. 'New Year?'

'I told you. In the car. We're having a barbie.'

Beth touched her brow. 'Yes, you did. Sorry. I'm really tired. Of course I'll be there.'

'Come on,' said Curtis, steering Angela towards the door. 'Time to leave Beth in peace.'

The moment Curtis and her mother left, loneliness descended. Beth was aware it was mostly fatigue but she'd become so accustomed to having Danny nearby that being alone felt wrong. Though she needed a shower, she needed his voice more.

It came over the phone like a hug. 'Hey, gorgeous sexy saddler girl. All settled?'

'Getting there. I've yet to unpack and I need a shower.'

'Wish I could have it with you.'

'I do too.' Beth wandered into her bedroom and began to pull dirty clothes from her suitcase and sort them into piles. 'I wish I didn't have to work tomorrow.'

'I wish you didn't either. If you didn't have that job, you'd still be here.'

Beth blinked as heat stung her eyes. She rubbed at them but still they itched. Tiredness, that's all it was. Tiredness and dismay at returning to a job she wasn't sure she could endure, at least for the short term.

'Beth?'

'Sorry. Having a moment.'

His voice lowered in sympathy. 'Yeah. I've had a few myself today.'

They chatted for a while longer, romantic words of longing and love padded with hope Beth wasn't sure she believed in, until Danny ordered her to shower, eat and sleep. Fatigued and hollowed out with sadness and doubt, Beth gave in without resistance.

As she climbed under the sheets, her bedroom's old air-conditioner rattling, Beth wondered what the hell she was doing here. The flat was hateful, her job not much better, and the weather oppressive, while across the country a man who loved her waited with his dreams and plans and faith that somehow they'd be all right.

But in the stuffy darkness of her room, with the looming weeks until she saw him again weighing heavy, 'all right' seemed a very long way off.

Beth spent New Year's Eve at Curtis's house surrounded by his and her mum's friends. She was surprised at how many they'd made. That the party would be dominated by Curtis's work mates she'd anticipated, but Beth had been startled by how chummy Angela was with their partners. Her mum had never been that outgoing in England and rarely entertained at home, yet here she acted as if this was normal. There was a lovely couple from her mum's pottery class too, and as the youngest there, it was Beth who seemed the friendless, odd one out.

'Having a nice time, darling?' asked her mum, clinking her glass against Beth's.

'I am. I didn't realise you'd made so many friends.'

'Most of them are Curtis's, but I've made a few.'

Beth studied her. She was dressed in a pretty summer skirt and simple top, and Roman sandals lacing up her legs. Her skin was tanned, her face lightly tinted with makeup, giving her a young, fresh look. The smile barely seemed to leave her face, and with every glance her mum directed Curtis's way, Beth felt the tug of recognition.

'You're so happy,' said Beth.

'I am, very.' Angela shot her a worried look. 'Aren't you?'

'I'm fine, Mum. Still finding my feet a bit, but I'll get there.'

Angela began to fuss. 'It's being alone in that pokey flat. You should move in with us. There's a spare room and we'd love to have you around.'

'Mum . . .'

'It'd save a lot of money too. Sydney's so expensive. I don't know how anyone is meant to get ahead, especially young people.'

'Mum,' said Beth, staying her with a hand on her arm, 'I'm fine.'

Angela blinked. 'I worry.'

'I know.' She hugged her carefully, mindful of their drinks. 'But you don't have to. I can manage.'

'I don't want you to manage, I want you to be happy.'

The words left Beth unable to speak and if it weren't for Curtis bounding over with a beer and a smile, she might have spilled her heart about Levenham and how she'd felt there. She let it go. A party wasn't the place for that kind of soul-baring.

The new year settled in. At the saddlery Beth was lumped with rug repairs. There were dozens of the rotten things and they seemed to have been stockpiled just for her, like some sort of punishment. It was tedious, itchy and smelly work, made worse by the oppressive heat and humidity blanketing the area. The workshop had no air-conditioning and by day's end, Beth's skin was rancid with horse hair and dust.

The urge to quit festered and grew, but Beth needed the money, and this time of year replacement jobs were few. She had to be careful too. The horsey world was tight-knit, people knew each other and talked. If she wanted another job near her mum, Beth had to keep her temper and maintain the quality of her work, no matter how trying the circumstances.

January passed achingly slow. Beth became bogged in routine. She went to work, sweated in the workshop, came home, ate, talked to Danny, sometimes read or watched a bit of telly, then went to bed. The two close girlfriends she'd made were both away enjoying summer holidays. Reprieve from boredom and loneliness came from Danny, who kept her entertained with messages and silly photos of himself, and pictures of his work, the pub, his family and cricket team. The local landscape in stunning shades of irrigated green and hayed-off blonde. He even sent photos of the saddlery. Every image made her almost ill with yearning.

Demand for her browbands continued in Levenham. Unwilling to take on such fiddly and time-consuming work, Grandpop turned the orders down but when Beth learned of the demand she asked him to take them on. That people were still chasing her design made her proud, plus the browbands helped kill the lonely night hours.

It was the second-last day of January when, after another purposeless day at work, Beth set down the rosette she was creating, and crossed to the back door of the flat and walked outside. She stared at the miserable yard, with its tiny clothes line, cracked concrete edging and forlorn lawn, and the flowers she'd planted that refused to thrive. Tilting her head back, she gazed at the darkening sky and emerging stars, and marvelled in a skyscape so different to what she'd grown up with.

It made her feel small.

It also made her question the choices she'd made.

There was a world out there, a universe. People who loved her. Opportunities. So why was she allowing herself to atrophy in this cheerless place?

She knew the answer: guilt. But her mum was happy now. She had friends, a man who adored her, a life stretching rich into the future. She didn't need Beth. And if she did, these days communication was instantaneous. Travel was accessible and relatively fast, even in a country the size of Australia. Her mum wouldn't be alone.

Beth paced, arms crossed tightly around herself as she mulled. Her mum wasn't the only issue, there was money. Unless the flat was re-rented immediately Beth would have to pay out her lease. Only a month, but that was money she didn't have. There were also relocation costs — utility bills to finalise, trailer hire, or perhaps storage if Beth decided to leave her things behind.

She stopped and looked again at the sky. It all seemed too much.

But maybe, just maybe that was her cowardice talking. Fear of the risk she'd be taking. She'd only known Danny a short time. Yes, they were in love now, but that didn't mean it would last.

He believed, though. He believed with every part of his big heart and honest soul.

Beth uncrossed her arms and dug her phone from her pocket. She stared at Danny's messages, at the photos, at hope.

Then she took a deep breath and dialled her mum's number. Forty minutes later, with her own hope rising, she phoned Grandpop. By the time she'd finished, Beth was grinning.

She'd promised Danny belief. Now he had it, and this time it was real.

Sixteen

Danny eyed his little sister across the kitchen table as he shovelled cereal into his mouth. From the stubborn set of her jaw, she was in one of her dangerous moods. Well, she could go right ahead because whatever mood Ebs was in, it had nothing on Danny's.

The day was fine, the weather forecast to be a very pleasant 28 degrees, and he was scheduled to spend the morning out on a local farm, checking a windmill installation — a job he normally enjoyed. But instead of waking in his usual sunny mood, Danny was tired and foul-tempered after yet another crap night's sleep, and more than a little panicky. He didn't know what he'd done or said but there was something wrong with Beth.

It had been more than three weeks since he'd sensed the change. It was like smoke creeping into the marrow of his bones and the fast-beating chambers of his heart — murky and elusive, but there. All through January Beth had been her usual self. Perhaps occasionally a bit down, but nothing that Danny felt he couldn't lift her out of.

Then the calendar flipped over to February and straight away he noticed a difference. At first it was subtle — Beth sounding distracted but otherwise normal — but as the days passed her distraction seemed to deepen until it morphed into borderline avoidance.

Beth used to answer his messages straight away, now he might wait an hour for a reply. In the past when they rang each other, they'd talk like they were the only two people in the world, sometimes late into the night. Now she sounded vague, almost remote, as if there were other things she'd rather be doing. Even more worryingly, Beth always seemed to be at her mum's. Out of all the signs, that one left him the most anxious. It was because of her mum that Beth couldn't see a way ahead for them.

Though conscious it made him sound desperate and weak, Danny asked over and over what was wrong, but Beth simply laughed and made excuses: she was tired, she was busy, he was fretting about nothing.

It wasn't nothing. He knew that for certain.

He had to get up there. And soon.

'I *said*,' Ebs smacked the table top, 'that you need to call in there today. At lunchtime.'

Danny frowned at his sister. 'I'm busy.'

Busy planning a trip north. This weekend, if he could get flights. It'd mean missing his cricket team's first finals match, but Beth was more important.

'You have to!'

'I don't have to do anything, Ebs. Get Mum to do it.'

Besides, Danny wasn't sure his aching heart would cope with walking into the saddlery.

'No!' She clenched her fists, face scrunching up.

Danny threw his mum an exasperated glance.

'Go on,' said Judy. 'It'll only take five minutes.'

'Why's it so crucial you have hoof oil today? I'm sure Hobbles' feet won't fall off if you miss one day of painting them.'

'Because!' Ebony huffed. 'It's *important*!'

'Jesus,' muttered Danny under his breath as he rose to rinse his bowl. As if he didn't have enough woman trouble.

'Well?' asked Ebs, crowding him at the sink.

'All right. If I can, I'll do it.'

'*No*, you have to *promise*.'

Worn down, Danny put his hands up in surrender. 'All right. I promise.'

Ebony clapped and hugged him. Bemused, he stroked her hair while shrugging at his mum, who simply nodded in approval, and smiled in a way that had Danny frowning again.

Women were bloody weird creatures.

🎁🎁🎁

There was only one car at the front of O'Brien's when Danny called in at twelve thirty. He'd almost not come, but guilt and dread of the teenage tantrum Ebs might pull if he broke his promise had him wolfing his sandwich down and rushing for the main street.

He parked and sat for a moment, staring at the front of

the shop as he fingered the plaited leather of his bracelet. Memories of Beth floated in his mind, thickening his throat. Wonderful times. Special times. Now he was scared shitless they'd never come again. Overwhelmed, Danny rested his head on the wheel and inhaled deeply for a moment, then puffing out a long breath, he unclipped his seatbelt and stepped outside.

John O'Brien was at the counter, flipping through the shop's order book.

'Hey, John,' called Danny, heading for the shelf where the hoof oil was kept. 'How you keeping these days?'

'Pretty well for an old fella. Yourself?'

'Not bad.' Which was a lie. Everything about the saddlery was worsening his panic over Beth. It had the comforting smell of her, of the things she loved. Once, he'd also been one of those things. What Danny meant to her now he had no idea. The worry of it was driving him crazy.

'Need a hand?' asked John.

'Nah, I'm fine. Ebs just wants some hoof oil.' Danny spotted the brand she'd asked for and picked it up, then turned for the counter.

And nearly dropped the tin.

'Hello, Danny.'

'Oh, Jesus. Beth.' For a long, long moment he could only stare and blink, then elation kicked in and he was almost running for the counter. The tin hit the top with a bang that Danny ignored. He clutched her face, searching it. Confused, overjoyed, incredulous. 'You're here.'

'Yes.'

'Oh, God.' He kissed her, then broke it off to press her close, his face buried in her neck, breathing the scent of her, her realness. Danny wanted to sob. He wanted to laugh. Instead he eased back to take her in, hands cradling her jaw. Disbelief and wonder filling him to the brim. 'Why didn't you tell me you were coming?'

'I wanted it to be a surprise.'

She was smiling and crying at the same time. Danny used his thumbs to wipe the tears from her cheeks and placed gentle kisses on the damp skin. 'How long are you here for?'

Beth glanced at John and her smile broadened. 'A while.'

His heartbeat hammered. He swallowed. 'What do you mean "a while"?'

'I've moved here. Grandpop has employed me in the shop, with the view of me taking over when he retires. I'll be living with Grandpop and Grandma until I get myself properly settled.'

'Moved? Here?' Danny knew he sounded like an idiot but her words were like scattered Scrabble tiles in his head. 'You mean permanently?'

Beth nodded.

'But I thought . . .' His breath was coming fast. Beth here? Forever? He couldn't seem to believe it, but the loving light in her eyes promised it was true. He hugged her again, making embarrassing groaning noises as he did. The past few weeks had been torture, and now this? The relief was incredible. *She* was incredible. 'What about your mum?'

'You were right. She only ever wanted me to be happy. And here is where I am happy. In Levenham, with Grandpop and Grandma, the saddlery.' Beth smiled shyly. 'And you.'

Danny couldn't take his eyes off her, or his hands. Or his lips. She was a dream made real. 'I can't believe it.'

'I can't either.' Her expression softened. 'I'm sorry for not telling you. I know you've been worried.'

'Why didn't you?'

'I wasn't sure it was going to work out. There was so much to organise and I was anxious about Mum. When I left the flat and moved in with her I kept fretting that she'd change her mind, but she didn't. She kept pushing me, telling me to take the chance, like she'd done with Curtis. Mum's been incredible. She even loaned me the money so I could do this.'

'I think I might like your mum.'

Beth laughed and poked him teasingly in the chest. 'I think she'll love you.'

'Not as much as I love *you*.'

'Love you more.'

Danny kissed her, ending the argument. When he resurfaced, Danny eyed the tin of hoof oil. 'So this is Squirt's doing again.'

'And your mother's.'

'Huh,' he said. There might be words when he arrived home tonight. Then again, he might not go home. A night in a motel room with Beth was looking very attractive right now.

'Don't be ungrateful. Ebony's matchmaking seemed to work all right last time.'

'Yeah, it did, didn't it?' Struck by a lightning bolt of

happiness, Danny grinned and lifted Beth off her feet, twirling her around. 'And look what it scored me: my own gorgeous sexy saddler girl.'

'While I scored my own hunky Santa. Best,' she said, smiling and pecking him playfully on the lips, 'Christmas.' Another, slightly longer brush of mouths. 'Ever.' This time the kiss didn't stop.

Best Christmas ever? Danny couldn't have agreed more.

Epilogue

Beth peered through the ute window and at her watch. 'What time did you say Melissa was coming?'

'Two.'

'She's late.'

Danny grinned at her. 'Impatient?'

'Yes.'

With good reason. Beth had a good feeling about this property. The dolomite and limestone bungalow was in dire need of renovation, but that hadn't put either of them off. She and Danny weren't averse to hard work, plus what the house lacked in modern amenities was more than made up for by its other assets. The property included 18 acres of slightly sloping land, perfectly situated on the north-eastern outskirts of Levenham and an easy drive to both their workplaces. Grazing land surrounded it on three sides, and research had shown there was no plans for rezoning. A rural idyll with a good chance of staying that way.

A car sounded along the road and pulled into the drive.

The real estate agent waved as she got out.

'Ready?' asked Danny.

'Definitely.'

He took her hand. 'Don't get your hopes up too much.'

Beth was trying not to, but want had lodged in her chest. Not for herself, but for Danny. He'd worked hard for this dream and she was desperate for him to have it.

They shook hands with Melissa, who made the usual small talk about the weather as she led them to the front door. It opened immediately. A short elderly lady with tightly curled grey hair, bird-like hands and a painful-looking stoop, beckoned them inside. She was well-dressed in slacks and a thin cardigan, and wearing lipstick and powder. Her frailty might be forcing her into a nursing home cottage in town, but she still had pride.

'Cup of tea?' Mrs Womersley asked, once introductions were made.

Danny and Melissa shook their heads.

'I'd love one,' said Beth, earning a delighted beam.

Mrs Womersley took Beth's arm, and with her free hand shooed Danny and Melissa off. 'You two look around while Beth and I chat.'

Danny raised an eyebrow at Beth, double-checking she was fine. Beth indicated with a smile that she was. They'd inspected a lot of properties over the last eight months, and if there was one thing she'd discovered it was that a good chat with the owner often yielded dividends. Danny had already pulled out of another potential purchase because Beth had wheedled out ongoing problems with a difficult neighbour.

Buying property had proved more trying than she'd ever imagined, but it was exciting too. All of life with Danny was exciting. Exciting, joyous and overloaded with love.

Mrs Womersley caught their silent exchange. 'Newlyweds?'

'Not yet. We're aiming for autumn but Danny wants to find a house first.' Beth lowered her voice. 'I think he has a thing about carrying me over the threshold.' In a fireman's lift, patting her bum — but Beth kept that to herself. 'He's a terrible romantic.'

Mrs Womersley's eyes sparkled as she chuckled. 'My David was the same. People think it's women who are made weak by love but the truth is, it's men. They're all big sooks inside. My boys are no different.'

Beth scanned the room as Mrs Womersley prepared tea, noting the many photographs and knick-knacks and children's drawings on the fridge. The layers of a well-lived life. 'You must have had some wonderful times here.'

'We did. I can show you, if you like.' At Beth's eager 'yes, please', she disappeared out of the room, returning moments later with a large photograph album. Mrs Womersley placed it on the table, then poured water into a teapot and brought it to the table. 'Let's reminisce while it brews.'

Settling companionably alongside Beth, she opened the first page and began to talk. And with every image, every story, Beth knew her good feeling was right.

'Well?' asked Danny when they were back at his car.

Beth was leaning against the wheel arch, smiling at the house. 'I like it.'

He raised an eyebrow. 'Just like?'

'Okay, I love it.'

He leaned with her. 'It's perfect. Well, not quite perfect. Bathroom and kitchen need a complete overhaul, but we knew that. It's a bit smaller than we want too, but we can always expand. It's not as if there isn't enough space.' He shifted in front of Beth and hoisted her easily onto the bonnet, and nestled close between her legs. Draping his arms around her waist, he looked up. Handsome, hopeful. 'What do you think, Beth? Want to make a home here with me?'

Beth stroked his hair, bursting with love for this man. 'Yes.'

'Good. I'll ring Melissa and talk offers this afternoon.'

She rested her chin on his head and regarded the house again. 'It has a chimney.'

'I saw.'

'We could play Santa games.'

Danny snuck a tickle to the underside of her breast. 'We could do a lot of things.'

Beth giggled and ducked to kiss him.

'Santa and the saddler.' He pressed his forehead against hers. 'What did I tell you? Christmas magic.'

'Except now it's all the time.'

'No, Beth,' said Danny, angling his head to kiss her again. 'Now it's forever.'

The End

Discover how Danny's friends Harry and Summer met in *Summer and the Groomsman*, available now in ebook and print from your favourite online retailer.

It's Levenham's wedding of the year but unlucky-in-love Harry Argyle has more on his mind than being groomsman.

After yet again nearly colliding with an escaped horse while driving home to the family farm, Harry Argyle comes face-to-face with its pretty owner, and doesn't hold back his disapproval.

Confronted by a bad-tempered giant on a dark country road, beautician and new arrival in town Summer Taylor doesn't know who to be more afraid for: herself or her darling horse Binky. It's not her fault Binky keeps escaping.

The alcoholic owner of the paddock she rents won't fix the fence and Binky can be sneaky when it comes to filling his stomach. But no matter how big and muscled the bully, she refuses to be intimidated.

When Harry's wedding party book a session at the day spa where Summer works, both she and Harry are horrified to be paired together. Grudgingly, they agree to make the most of it - only for the session to spiral into disaster. Realising he's made a dill of himself in front of sweet Summer yet again, Harry vows to set things right.

Summer isn't about to easily forgive the man who called her horse stupid, no matter how brave and kind, but with everyone on Harry's side, even fate, resistance is hard. Can these two find love or will Summer's wayward horse put his hoof in it again?

If you'd like to know when my next release comes available plus gain access to exclusive content, news and giveaways, and a couple of sweet short stories to enjoy over a cuppa, please sign up to my newsletter at cathrynhein.com.

Dear Reader

Thank you so much for buying and reading *Santa and the Saddler*. I had such a lovely time writing this book and hope you enjoyed Beth and Danny's journey to love and happiness as much as I did.

If you'd like to know when my next release comes available plus gain access to exclusive content, news and giveaways, please sign up to my newsletter. You can also connect via Facebook and Twitter using @CathrynHein. For all my social media links and more information about me and my books, including the inspiration behind *Santa and the Saddler*, along with plenty of other fun stuff, simply visit me at cathrynhein.com.

Help others find their next read by leaving a review of this novella on your favourite book website.

*

My other rural-set romances include:

Wayward Heart
April's Rainbow
Summer and the Groomsman
The Falls
Rocking Horse Hill
Heartland
Heart of the Valley
Promises

Romantic Adventure:
The French Prize